PURE
HEROINE

BY: KEISHA ERVIN

DEDICATION

This book is dedicated to all of the people who have been riding with me since 2004… NIGGA WE MADE IT!!!!

MUTHAFUCKAS
NEVER LOVED US.
-DRAKE, "WORST
BEHAVIOR"

CHAPTER 1

"Where are these heffas at?" Kelly thought to herself, checking her watch.

She'd been sitting at her favorite restaurant in New York, Le Cirque, for thirty minutes awaiting her girlfriends', Meesa and Destiny's, arrival. Kelly loved Le Cirque. Experts across the country voted it the best restaurant in the world. Le Cirque was a New York staple and had been around since 1974. The nostalgic ambiance of the restaurant made you feel at home and the gourmet dishes were to die for.

If they're not here within five minutes, I'm up, she thought.

It was August in Manhattan and the weather was absolutely gorgeous. Looking out of the window, Kelly tried to see if she could spot the girls anywhere. Then she spotted Meesa and Destiny walking through a crowd of people looking as if they'd stepped directly off the runway. Both women were FIERCE! Meesa always stayed on point with her look.

She was the CEO and head designer of Miss A, a clothing company she'd created in her apartment when they lived in St. Louis. Since its launch, Miss A had grown to be a billion dollar company. Outside of apparel, they'd branched off into handbags, shoes and home décor. Women all over the world wore Meesa's designs and Miss A was in every major department store from Bergdorf's to Neiman Marcus. When Hollywood's most sought after starlets wanted something hot to rock on the red carpet they called on Meesa.

Even the small screen loved her. Meesa was currently filming her very own reality show for the Style Network. While Meesa was the creative force behind Miss A, Destiny was the face of the company. She was Meesa's muse and since Miss A's debut in 2004, she'd gone on to be a world-renowned supermodel.

But the glue that held the company together was Kelly. She was the head of sales and distribution. All of the women, including their other friends Gwyn and Nikki, had been girls since as far back as either of them could remember. They'd gone through hell and back with one another.

They'd survived cheating spouses, abusive relationships, shootouts, the death of their friend Tamara and even an attempt on Meesa's life by Destiny's deranged ex-boyfriend. But through it all, they stood strong and now were rich and successful. As Meesa and Destiny walked past the restaurants window, the two women blew Kelly a kiss and waved. Instead of waving back, Kelly hit them both with the middle finger and rolled her eyes.

"Took y'all long enough. Can y'all ever get anywhere on time?" She griped as they sat down and the camera crew hovered over them.

"You know, workaholic here," Destiny said pointing over at Meesa. "had to put the finishing touches on her spring/summer collection before we left out. On top of that, she changed her lipstick color like three times."

Kelly looked over at Meesa and smiled. Despite the attention she received from the camera crew following her every move, Meesa still stood out in the crowd. She was a bombshell. She was short and petite but her platinum blond, pixie cut hair, hazel-green eyes and heart-shaped lips set her apart from other women. She was an extraordinary beauty but she didn't let her good looks go to her head.

"Remember work comes before play, ladies," Meesa smirked, crossing her legs. "And plus, we made an impromptu stop by DVF. I had to get this top they had on a mannequin in the window."

"Did you order yet?" Destiny asked Kelly.

"No, I'm not inconsiderate like you two bitches," she answered.

"Oh, bitch, get over it," Destiny laughed, pulling out her Chanel compact mirror.

"Whatever." Kelly waved her off.

"Well, I don't know about y'all but I'm starving," Meesa said, as a waiter approached their table.

Once their orders were placed, the women sat back and chit chatted.

"So, Meesa, are you ready for Fashion Week this year?" Kelly asked, trying her best to forget that the cameras were there.

"Yeah, I'm hella excited," Meesa replied, rubbing her hands together. "Our show will be September 10th. You know Mina, Victor, the kids, my dad and my step-mom are gonna be there."

"No, I didn't." Kelly broke off a piece of bread and dipped it into olive oil.

"Yep," Meesa nodded.

"You haven't seen them in a minute; have you?"

"Nope, but I talk to Mina on the phone like every day though."

"What about Ed?" Destiny asked.

"I talk to him maybe once a week. You know it's weird 'cause all of my life I've wanted to know who my father was, and now that I know him, I don't know how I should feel even after all these years."

"Well, girl, that's natural. I wouldn't know how to feel either," Kelly agreed.

"We'll see how things go when they arrive," Meesa shrugged.

"Enough about that." Destiny flicked her wrist bored with the conversation.

"I can't wait to strut my stuff down the catwalk. 'Cause you know bitches be hatin'. But it's all good 'cause I will never get tired of people telling me how beautiful I am." Destiny gloated looking at herself in the mirror again.

"You are one conceited ho," Kelly laughed, shaking her head.

"Don't hate me because I'm beautiful." Destiny blew herself a kiss and smoothed down her hair.

"You're right. You're the best lookin' gay guy here," Kelly joked, cracking up laughing.

"Whateva." Destiny popped her lips as their food arrived. "Who is that dude over there? He has been staring at us since we got here."

"Who?" Meesa searched the room.

"The cutie over there with the low cut." Destiny pointed her head in the dude's direction.

"Oh, I see him. He got on a white, V-neck tee. He's cute but my nigga at home look better," Meesa declared, taking a bite of her tuna tartare.

"He kind of reminds me of the rapper Nas," Kelly added.

"He does, doesn't he?" Destiny agreed.

"Mmm hmm," Kelly eye fucked him from across the room. "I wonder is he single 'cause my vagina happens to be free," she joked.

"Girl, please, Jayden got yo' ass sewed up," Destiny teased.

"Right," Kelly replied. "I know one thing though, if he keeps on staring like I'm something he wanna eat, I'ma go over there and drop this thang down on him."

"Too late; he's coming over." Meesa situated herself in her seat.

"Excuse me, ladies." The guy nervously looked at the women and the camera crew.

"I don't mean to bother you but I had to tell you." He focused on Destiny. "You are absolutely breathtaking."

"Thank you. I get that all the time," she grinned, sticking out her tongue.

"Have you ever done a video before?"

"Is this nigga tryin' to get me to do a porno?" Destiny looked back and forth between her girlfriends. "'Cause I mean, I experimented back in my twenties but those days are over." She popped her lips.

"No, no." The guy laughed. "I mean a music video."

"Oh no, I'm a model, sweetie." Destiny swung her long weave to the side and batted her eyelashes.

"Everybody's a model in this city." The guy replied, mockingly.

"Excuse me but who are you again?" Meesa questioned, annoyed.

"My bad. My name is Dre." He extended his hand for a shake.

"Well, Dre, I'm Meesa." She shook his hand. "And this is Kelly. I'm the owner and designer of Miss A. Destiny is the face of my collection and ad campaign. What do you do for a living, Dre?"

"I knew I saw your face before." Dre said to Destiny. "I'm a manager. I manage a rapper by the name of Cash. Have you heard of him?"

"Ah duh, I love his music. He be getting the club crunk." Destiny booty popped in her seat. "Does anybody still say crunk?"

"No," Meesa laughed.

"Yeah, Cash just got done recording his new album. We're going to shoot the video for his first single in a couple of weeks. I would love it if you were the lead girl in the video."

"If the pay is right and the clothes are tight I'm there." Destiny snapped her fingers.

"Bet. Well here's my card. Tell your agent to give me a call so we can talk things over."

"I sure will." Destiny took his card and smiled.

"It was a pleasure meeting you ladies. Have a nice day." Dre winked his eye at Kelly before leaving.

"You too," Meesa said, dryly, rushing him along.

"Is it just me or did he just wink at me?" Kelly asked, perplexed.

"It was just you," Destiny teased. "Nah, I'm just playin'. Homeboy was checkin' you out, girl."

"I don't know about him y'all; something ain't right." Meesa shook her head from side to side with a nervous look on her face.

"Girl, calm yo' ole scary ass down. You think something wrong wit' everybody we meet since that stuff with Daryl went down." Destiny rolled her eyes.

"You damn right. I don't wanna die yet. At least not until Love and Hip Hop gets canceled," Meesa said with a laugh.

After having lunch with the girls, Kelly took a cab home. She stayed about ten minutes away from Meesa and Gwyn in Tribeca, New York. Miss A's headquarters was in the Meatpacking District and Kelly loved venturing out to that part of the city every day to work. It gave her the perfect opportunity to get away from her child's father and their problems. Ever since her and her fiancé, Jaden, moved to New York, they'd been experiencing problems.

The move up North was supposed to better their situation but it seemed to only make matters worse. Financially they were straight since Kelly worked for Meesa. Working for Miss A she made more money in a year's time than she had made in her entire life.

Back home in St. Louis Jaden was the primary bread winner. He made his money the best way he knew how - by selling dope. He thought when they moved to New York that things would pop off for him quickly in the drug game, but it didn't. With Black out of the game, being in a new city with no connects made for hard times. Jaden suddenly became the stay-at-home parent while Kelly worked a 9-to-5 paying all of the bills.

She understood that for him to be a black man without a job had to hurt his pride and manhood but him not having a job wasn't her fault. Nobody told him to hug the block all day with his friends. He could have easily gone to college with Kelly if he had wanted to. But Jaden was too busy ripping and running the streets with his friends to worry about school. Now in his 30's, the effects of him never working a 9-to-5 were taking its toll. The only thing Kelly wanted was for her and Jaden to get things back on track but as the days passed, that dream seemed to be fading fast.

To Kelly's dismay, as soon as she entered through the front door of her house the smell of marijuana hit her smack dab in the face. Instantly she was annoyed. When she walked into the living room she found Jaden sitting on the couch in a wife beater, sweat pants, socks and house shoes. He had one leg propped up on the coffee table while he played 2K14. Miller High Life beer cans were everywhere and cigar fillings were scattered on the couch, table and floor. Placing her vintage Dior bag down, Kelly cleared her throat to let him know that she was in the room.

"What's up, baby?" He spoke while chugging down another beer.

"I think I need to be askin' you that question." Kelly snapped, running her hands through her long length locs.

She was so fed up with his bullshit.

"Don't come home with that shit today, man. I ain't in the mood," Jaden sneered.

"From the looks of this house, it don't look like you in the mood to do shit!" Kelly yelled while surveying her surroundings.

The dishes from that morning were still sitting in the sink. None of the trash cans had been emptied and Jaden Jr. was nowhere to be found.

"Jaden? Where is my son?! You mean to tell me that you haven't gone and got him from preschool yet?" She asked ready to explode.

"Aww damn, my bad, I forgot." He sat up and put the game on pause.

"How you gon' forget to get yo' own damn son? I can't believe you! That's the only thing I asked you to do and you can't even do that! As a matter-of-fact, what have you done all day?"

"I called a few places to see if they had any job openings."

"Okay and what did they say?" Kelly crossed her arms across her chest.

"All of the places were hiring but the pay wasn't shit." Jaden said, now back concentrating on the game.

"How much was the pay, Jaden?"

"The lowest was thirteen dollars an hour and the highest was twenty."

"And you turned that down?" Kelly said in disbelief.

"Yeah, that shit was chump change compared to what I'm used to making on the streets," he shrugged.

"Have you lost your goddamn mind? You ain't on the block no more! Do you know how many people out here are dying to even get a job, let alone one paying twenty dollars an hour?"

"I hear you but I ain't gon' settle for no bullshit. In New York, twenty dollars an hour is chump change."

"Wow... I can't even talk to you right now! I'm gettin' ready to go get my son!" Kelly snatched up her purse.

"You want me to go with you?" Jaden looked over his shoulder at her.

"No, just sit yo' ass there and finish playin' that tired-ass video game!" She yelled, slamming the door behind her.

Two weeks later Meesa and Destiny stood on the set of Cash's new music video *Too Turnt.* Destiny could hardly breathe as she fanned herself with her hand. She'd just gotten done dancing her heart out while standing in front of Cash as he rapped the words to his booty shaking, end of summer anthem. Destiny had on nothing but a black bra and a pair of black, leather, booty shorts but wardrobe made sure to lace her with about $200,000 worth of diamonds.

"Get it, bitch! You worked that shit!" Meesa exclaimed, giving her girl props.

"Thank you but I'm tired as hell," Destiny huffed.

"I just saw the playbacks and you look great on camera."

"I saw it too. Your skin looks flawless, mama." The male makeup artist, Anton, said touching up her face.

"Girl, Kat is gon' go crazy when he sees this shit," Destiny said, fearing the worse.

"This is strictly business. Kat will understand. He knows good and well that you are his woman," Meesa guaranteed.

"Now I on the other hand would have a problem because Black crazy ass ain't having it. He would kill everybody up in here."

"So what you think of Cash?" Destiny asked, taking a sip of water.

"He seems a'ight I guess; why?"

"Have you looked at that nigga? He is *fine*." Destiny gave her mock-glare and grinned.

"I have a man at home who ain't trying to be gangsta. He is gangsta, ok? I ain't got time to be fawning over some wannabe thug." Meesa screwed up her face.

"Wannabe thug, huh?" She heard a male voice say from behind.

Embarrassed as hell, Meesa realized that Cash was standing directly behind her and had overheard everything.

"Please tell me that you didn't just hear that?" Meesa closed her eyes and winced.

"If I said I didn't, then I would be lying." He smiled showing off a perfect set of thirty-twos.

"I am so sorry." Meesa spun around to face him. "That was totally uncalled for and very unprofessional of me. Please forgive me," she pleaded.

"You good, li'l mama. People say shit like that all the time. Ain't no Rick Ross'in over here. Trust me; I ain't no studio thug."

"I'm sure they do." Destiny mumbled, fanning herself but for all different reasons now.

"Look, my album drops next week. I would love it if you two would attend my record release party."

"Can we bring some friends of ours?" Meesa quizzed.

"That's cool. The more, the merrier."

"Bet. We'll be there." Destiny cheesed like a groupie.

"Cash and Destiny, back to your places please." The 1st AD yelled through the bullhorn.

"A'ight, ladies and gents." Destiny stood up and fixed her shorts. "Time for me to go shake my ass for some cash."

FUCK IT THO, HE ON
ME.
-CHRISS ZOE,
"HOMEBOY"

CHAPTER 2

The following week all of the girls, including their men, piled into a black stretch limousine to attend Cash's record release party. Kelly was the only one riding solo. After their blow-up, she had been giving Jaden the silent treatment. She didn't want him anywhere near her so she left him at home. The party was huge and all of the who's who of the entertainment industry would be there.

Each of the ladies was dressed to the nines in designer labels. Kelly's locs were down with a crimp in them and she wore a green DKNY dress and heels. Destiny, the Tika Sumpter look-alike, had eighteen inch weave sewn into her hair and wore a beaded, Versace mini dress. Nikki's crème, Gucci shift dress melted into her skin and her big, curly, honey blonde hair framed her face.

Her sun-kissed, freckled skin glowed under the night sky. Gwyn, the diva of all divas, had to outshine everybody by wearing a backless, black, Alice + Olivia dress and black, stiletto, Gucci heels. Meesa, the risk taker of the group, wore her short platinum blonde hair in soft curls. The black, Ray-Ban wafer shades and big, gold earrings she rocked framed her oval face perfectly. The rest of her outfit consisted of a black bandeau top, 60's printed dancing skirt and five and a half inch Charlotte Olympia heels.

As they pulled up to the club, paparazzi were everywhere. All of the girls got out first so that Destiny could make her grand entrance. Meesa and Black stood in front of the step and repeat and posed for the slew of photographers. Meesa couldn't get over how handsome her husband looked. In her eyes Black was the sexiest man on Earth. His coffee colored skin and full beard was tantalizing. Since their move from St. Louis, he'd cut his locs off only to grow them again.

Black exuded confidence and swag like no other. He was a great father and an even better husband and friend. He'd been a huge supporter of her career but unbeknownst to any of their friends, Meesa and Black had begun to have marital problems. She thought by now they would be straight. Hell, their relationship had already endured enough. They'd survived him cheating on her, Meesa almost losing her life and him retiring from the drug world still in one piece.

But lately, Black had begun to grow distant and quiet. Whenever they were together it seemed like his mind was somewhere else. Meesa tried everything to bring him out of his funk but nothing seemed to work. She just prayed that the vacation she planned for them after Fashion Week would boost their relationship.

"Baby, can you please pull up your pants. Sagging is so ghetto. You're a grown-ass fuckin' man. Act like it," Meesa griped as she and Black posed for the cameras.

Black rolled his eyes and lifted his pants some.

"Meesa, can we get a picture of you alone?" The photographers yelled.

"Of course," She agreed cheerfully. "Babe, you don't mind do you?" She said, already posing for a solo pic.

"Nah, I'ma just go inside." Black backed away, annoyed.

In the beginning playing the background to his wife wasn't a problem. But over the last couple of years, he'd grown tired of being Mr. Meesa. It was bad enough she was always working and he was basically a stay-at-home dad. The reality show she was filming was making things even worse. Black missed his old neighborhood, his pot'nahs, making transactions and being the man in the streets. He yearned for the notoriety and the fame. Yes, he'd promised his wife that he'd leave the streets behind but being a celebrity wasn't for him. He was a street nigga to the heart and one day Meesa would have to accept that.

Inside the 40/40 Club the place was packed with people. All of the hottest rappers, R&B singers, actors and athletes were in the spot. If you were looking to snag a baller this was the place to be. Gwyn immediately caught attention because the girl had the nerve to bring her courier dog, Ferragamo, to the star-studded event.

She swore up and down that she couldn't part with the dog for a second. Nobody could stand her dog. He barked and snarled at everybody he came in contact with. Gwyn had already been a mess before they all became rich but now the chick was simply off the chain. Money had done the girl some justice though. As soon as she got to New York she went and got the best weave job she could find. She also had her teeth whitened and her boobs done. Thankfully, she had a little sense left and opted for a small D instead of big 'ole jalopy titties like Pamela Anderson.

As if Destiny being vain wasn't enough, now they had Gwyn to put up with too. Her attitude, conceitedness and smart mouth were too much for one person to handle. Nobody could knock her though because she did look good. On numerous occasions, it had been said that she looked like a younger version of Kimora Lee Simmons. After that,

Gwyn really lost her mind and began demanding the star treatment wherever she went.

"Garcon!" She yelled, waving her hand in the air to get the waiter's attention.

The camera crew was there filming their every move.

"If you don't quit being ghetto," Kelly nudged her. "Unless you wanna wait in line at the bar, I suggest you wait until he makes it across the room."

"Bitch, please, I'm thirsty."

"Girl, ain't that Jay-Z standing over there by the bar?" Nikki asked star-struck.

"Ooooh is Beyoncé here with him?" Kelly wondered out loud. "'Cause if she is I'm gonna spazz the fuck out."

"If she's anything like me, then she ain't letting that nigga go nowhere without her. As much money as he got, if I were her, I would have a tracking device on his ass. His ass wouldn't be able to move ten feet without me tracking his ass down." Gwyn declared making the girls laugh.

"Ain't that the guy Dre over there talking to Vanessa Simmons?" Meesa asked.

"Yeah, that's him." Kelly answered, spotting him.

"Girl, he is fine." Nikki chimed in.

"He is, isn't he?" Kelly said salivating too.

"Damn right he's fine. You better be a woman about yours and get on that," Gwyn suggested.

"Have you forgotten that I have a man sitting at home?" Kelly looked at her like she was crazy.

"Exactly!" Gwyn rolled her neck. "That nigga sitting at home with no money, no job, no car, no nothin'! Girl, you better quit playin' and get wit a big dick nigga that can beat the pussy up right and take care of you and yo' son. Ain't nobody got time to be dealing with no broke-ass nigga."

"I love Jaden, Gwyn. It ain't that easy for me to just turn off my feelings like you."

"Look, Kelly, a man ain't good but for a couple of things and that's paying yo' bills, fucking you real good and spoiling you with gifts. And if he can't do that, then you need to drop his ass." Gwyn stated adamantly.

Spotting a waiter she quickly took a glass of champagne off the tray as the waiter walked by.

"I guess," Kelly sighed.

"No, honey, you know because a nigga ain't shit. You are too old to be puttin' up wit a bunch of nonsense," Gwyn countered.

"Don't listen to her, Kelly." Meesa wrapped her arm around her friend. "You know she's only saying that because her ass is still bitter from her break up with Trey."

"Whatever. You ain't even have to go there." Gwyn scowled taking a sip of champagne.

"Just look at me and Black, Kelly." Meesa smiled over at her husband who was across the room talking to Kat.

"We've had our fair share of ups and downs but we made it through. I know in my heart that you and Jaden can do the same."

"Girl fuck what ya' heard. You better listen to me," Gwyn advised.

"I'm through with the whole entire conversation. Come on, Meesa, let's go get us some sushi." Kelly pulled her away by the arm.

Once Meesa was out of ear listening distance, Gwyn stated, "I am so sick and tired of hearing about Meesa and Black."

"I thought it was just me," Nikki laughed.

"Don't get me wrong. Meesa is my girl and all but damn, don't nobody feel like hearing that shit all the time."

"Yeah, it does get aggravating after a while."

"Everybody ain't gon' find a man like Black. Shit, we'll be lucky if we find a man like OJ," Gwyn laughed.

"Girl, you are crazy," Nikki giggled.

"Come on let's go get another drink." Gwyn took Nikki by the hand.

As they made their way through the mob of celebrities, publicists, managers and contest winners, Gwyn thought back on the comment that Meesa made. She had in fact been bitter towards men since her breakup with Trey Songz. She hadn't planned on falling in love with him but once she did she knew that she would never love like that again. Trey took her heart on an emotional roller coaster ride and it took Gwyn three years to finally get off. Since then, the word love hasn't crossed her mind or lips. Gwyn was about one thing, making money.

Since Trey she'd dated some of the wealthiest men in the United States. They would take her on expensive shopping sprees and fly her to some of the most exotic locations in the world. Gwyn thought that having money and power would make her happy. But having all the glitz and glamour in the world wouldn't keep her safe and secure at night. As Gwyn reached for another glass of champagne, she felt the soft touch of someone grab her hand.

"Weren't you in Meek Mill's last video?" A random guy with a thick New York accent and bulging biceps asked.

"Back up, Jersey Shore," Gwyn lightly pushed his chest.

"Damn." The cutie smiled. "Why I gotta be all that?"

"Do I look like a video ho to you?" Gwyn snapped, insulted.

"Nah, but you damn sure look good enough to eat," Cash smiled, admiring her frame.

"Who are you?" Gwyn eyed him up and down.

"Don't play wit me; you know exactly who I am." Cash licked his bottom lip.

"Ewww, boy, bye," she scowled. "Go play."

"How you gon' come to somebody's party and not even know who the party is for?"

"I know whose party this is. It's Cash's album release party. What you supposed to be Cash?" Gwyn looked him up and down.

"As a matter-of-fact, I am." He gazed deep into her eyes.

"Well, I'm Gwyn. Gwyneth Lee, vice president of marketing and promotions for Miss A." She extended her perfectly manicured hand and gave him her card.

"Oh, so, you're Meesa and Destiny's girl?"

"Yeah and this is my girl Nikki."

"Nice to meet you. Let me introduce you to my nigga OJ," Cash got his pot'nah's attention.

OJ couldn't even get out hello before the girls broke out laughing.

"What's so funny?" Cash asked confused.

"Oh nothin'; just a li'l inside joke." Gwyn and Nikki smiled at one another.

"Anyway, shorty, you got style. I like that." Cash admired her curvaceous frame.

"You ain't telling me nothin' I don't already know," Gwyn replied with a smirk.

Walking up on her, Cash whispered into her ear, "Come home with me tonight?"

"You can't be serious?" Gwyn said taken aback.

"I never joke when it comes to something I want."

"I don't even know you."

"Then get to know me." Cash whispered into her ear.

He was so close to her that Gwyn's breasts were pressed up against his rock solid chest. She suddenly felt weak. She hadn't felt that way in years.

"I'll pass." Gwyn shook her head, trying her best to seem unfazed.

"Can't say a nigga didn't try." Cash stepped back, disappointed.

"Next time try harder," Gwyn countered.

"I will." He smiled walking away leaving Gwyn flustered.

"Excuse my man. Success has gone to that nigga's head," OJ laughed.

"It's okay," Nikki blushed. "It's gone to hers too."

Sensing some major chemistry between the two, Gwyn excused herself. With a drink in her hand, she peeped Cash from across the room. He was everything that she had been trying to avoid these last couple of years. He was too cute for words and arrogant as hell. Just looking at him made her want to moan '*Ooh, Papi*'.

Like her, Cash was Asian and black. His creamy, butter colored complexion, almond shaped eyes, hoop nose ring, kissable lips and goatee caused her pussy to cream. All of his hair except for the top was shaved low. His hair at the top was slicked back into a pompadour. On the right side of his head was a tattoo of a lion. In each of his ears were nickel sized gauges.

Cash's neck, back, chest and arms were covered in tattoos. He looked to be about six feet tall with a very well built body. Cash caught Gwyn's eye. They both gazed at one another. Gwyn stopped their staring contest by rolling her eyes at him. Afterwards she headed back towards Nikki. Cash laughed at her immaturity and continued his conversation.

"So can I call you some time, Nikki?" OJ probed.

"I would love that."

"Dang, y'all still over here cakin'?" Gwyn asked jokingly.

"We were until you rudely interrupted us. Excuse her, OJ. She don't know no better," Nikki grinned.

"It's cool. I'm about to head out anyway but I'm gon' holla at you later, a'ight?" OJ caressed the side of her face.

"Okay," Nikki smiled as he walked away. "Damn he is fine."

"He, a'ight," Gwyn grimaced.

"Bitch, don't hate."

"What? The nigga look a'ight." Gwyn shrugged her shoulders.

"You know damn well he look better than a'ight."

"Okaaaaaaaaay you lucked up and found you a winner. You happy now?"

"It's okay, you gon' find you a man one day too," Nikki joked.

"I don't need a man. All I need is a black American Express card, boo boo."

"That's why yo' ass is lonely and bitter now."

"Whatever. Where is Meesa and them at?" Gwyn searched the room for them.

"There they are over there," Nikki pointed. "C'mon."

Both women walked over to their friends and joined in on their conversation.

"You having fun, babe?" Meesa looked up at Black.

"It's cool." He answered not even bothering to look in her direction. "I'm ready to bounce. Why don't we leave here and hit the strip club?"

"I'm down," Gwyn raised her hand.

Everyone else agreed as well except for Meesa and Kelly.

"Y'all can go. I am not going to no damn strip club. What I look like?" Meesa turned up her face. "That shit is fuckin' disgusting and Black, I really don't want you to go either. You're married. What you need to go to the strip club for?"

"'Cause it's fun." He looked at her like she was dumb.

"Nah, I don't think so."

"Whatever, man," He replied annoyed.

"Destiny, you wanna stay here don't you? I know you're having fun." Meesa tried to play off her husbands' rude behavior.

"Girl, I am having a ball," Destiny smiled brightly, loving all of the attention that she was getting.

"I see," Gwyn said with an attitude.

"What is her problem?" Meesa asked.

"Guess who tried to holla at Miss Thang over here?" Nikki said.

"Who?"

"Mr. Cash himself," Nikki announced to everyone.

"What?!" The girls exclaimed.

"Yes, but check it, her stuck up ass turned him down," Nikki laughed.

"You got to be kidding me," Destiny said astonished.

"I sure did," Gwyn spoke up. "Look, just 'cause his ass got a couple of hit records don't mean shit. He's just like any other man I've ever met. He thinks with his dick and not his brain and I ain't got time to deal with that shit."

"You's a good one 'cause even I would have hit that," Kelly smiled.

"Uh ah, y'all ain't noticed that Miss Thang ain't said a word about trickin' no dough outta his ass?" Meesa pointed out.

"You're right, Meesa, usually she would have been all over him by now," Nikki concluded.

"*Gweeeeeen got a crush,*" Meesa sang.

"Kiss my ass, Meesa." Gwyn stormed off annoyed.

"Don't be getting mad at me 'cause you *looove* Cash!" Meesa continued to tease.

"Shut up!" Gwyn yelled over her shoulder as she walked away.

"Tell me which color you like the best?" Meesa asked, holding up two sample swatches.

"The crème one," Gwyn answered, barely looking up from her paperwork.

"Heffa, you ain't even look up." Meesa dropped her hands down to her side.

"I did. The crème one looks better."

"Have you talked to Kelly today?"

"No she's probably somewhere running in behind Jaden's ole trifling ass," Gwyn scoffed. "I will be glad when she drops his tired ass."

"Now, why you gotta go there?" Meesa asked, trying her best not to laugh.

"'Cause, it's the truth," Gwyn chuckled. "He is so wack now."

"Excuse me, Miss Lee, but these just came for you." Gwyn's personal assistant said handing her a bouquet of flowers filled with Hydrangeas and Lilies of the Valley.

"Ooooooooooh… you got flowers, bitch! Who sent you those?" Meesa tried her best to peek over her shoulder and see the name on the card.

"Back up, li'l nosey-ass girl." Gwyn elbowed her. "I don't know which one of my niggas sent them."

To her surprise, the flowers were from Cash.

"Yasssssss, Cash on dat ass!" Meesa slapped her hard on the butt.

"You are way too excited," Gwen frowned. "Calm yo' ass down."

"Just shut up and tell me what the damn card says!"

"It says, 'let your guard down and take a chance on a nigga. XO, Cash. P.S. A car is waiting for you downstairs.'"

"Girl, he sent a car for you." Meesa ran over to the window.

Sure enough there was a black Escalade parked out front.

"Girl, he really does have a car waiting for you," Meesa exclaimed.

"Ok and?" Gwyn threw the card and flowers in the trash.

"You have lost yo' damn mind," Meesa retrieved the flowers from the trash. "You know how expensive these flowers are?"

"I know and I don't care," Gwyn shot dismissively.

"So you mean to tell me you not gon' go?" Meesa looked at her as if she were crazy.

"No. I'm not getting ready to jump 'cause this nigga sent me some punk-ass flowers and a car service."

"You are such a bitch. If you don't get yo' ass outta here and go meet that man."

"No, I don't know where he's trying to take me. What if he's a killer?"

"Like that's ever stopped you before." Meesa shot sarcastically.

"My mama always told me not to get in random cars wit' strangers," Gwyn opposed.

"Gwyn, leave!" Meesa handed her purse to her. "The driver is waiting for you."

"Write down the license plate number in case this nigga be on some funny shit and try to kill me," Gwyn ordered.

"Ok-ok-ok; now go." Meesa pushed her out the door.

Gwyn reluctantly left the building and walked outside to the car. A nice, white gentleman was waiting to open the door for her.

"Good afternoon, ma'am."

"Hi." She spoke getting into the backseat.

She didn't know what the hell she was doing. She had no interest in pursuing Cash. He was just another rapper. She'd been there and done that too many times to count. But there was something about him that intrigued her. *Fuck it,* Gwyn thought. *At best you might get a free meal outta this.* To her dismay, seconds later she was being whisked away to an undisclosed location.

Back inside the building Meesa placed Gwyn's flowers in a vase. Little did she know, she had her own surprise on the way. Black walked into Gwyn's office and found her. Whenever Black came to the office, which was rare, all of the employees, including some of the men, swooned.

Black was sexy as fuck. He and the rapper Wale could've been twins. Black was just taller and buffer. He stayed fresh to death in the latest fashions. That day he donned a pair of brown Aviator shades, a thin, gold, rope chain, Kill Brand red, white and blue tank top, cargo pants and Tims.

"What's up, baby?" He wrapped his arms around her waist and kissed her neck from behind.

"Not in the office, babe," She pushed him back with her butt. "My employees might see you."

"And? Damn, you act like you're not happy to see me," he grimaced.

Meesa turned and faced him.

"I'm always happy to see you," she replied, noticing that his right forearm was covered in gauze and plastic wrap.

"Black, what have you done now?" She asked already annoyed.

"I went and got a new tattoo," he smiled brightly.

"Of what? What did you get this time?"

"A picture of Jesus' face on my forearm."

"Don't you think you have enough tattoos?"

"Apparently not if I got another one." Black shot back becoming frustrated.

This wasn't what he came to see her for. He'd come because he missed her and needed to talk to her. He didn't come for her to bitch at him the whole entire time.

"I'll be glad when you are over all of this ghetto bullshit," Meesa shot sarcastically.

"I'll be glad when you find something to do besides complain." Black declared having had enough of her stank attitude. "Look, I did come up here 'cause I missed you but now you've ruined that. I need to holla at you about something important."

"Ok." Meesa led him to her office and closed the door behind them.

The camera crew stood around them filming their entire conversation.

"What you need to talk to me about?" Meesa took a seat on the couch.

"I just got a call from my old dude today."

"For real? What he want?"

"Meesa, can you scoot over a little? The lighting where you are isn't good," Ian, the producer of her show, said.

"Sure," Meesa scooted over and posed perfectly.

"Resume," Ian instructed.

Black ice grilled Ian. He was sick of the cameras and he was sick of Ian interrupting their life just to get a scene for Meesa's stupid-ass reality show.

"He's getting out of jail in a few weeks," Black continued speaking.

"That's good," Meesa smiled with her legs crossed.

"That's not it though."

"What else is there?"

"He needs a place to stay."

Meesa sat still and looked at Black with a blank stare on her face.

"I know you don't think he's coming to stay with us?" She finally responded.

"Come on, Meesa, that's my father. I can't just leave him out on the streets."

"Black, we don't know that man from a can of paint. Ain't no way in hell he coming up in my house!"

"Your house? You lost yo' fuckin' mind? Don't let these cameras get you fucked up. The last time I checked it was my house too. I do pay the bills up in that muthafucka or have you forgotten?"

"Cut the cameras off." Meesa demanded taking her mic pack off.

"But—" Ian tried to stop her.

"No buts. Out!" Meesa pushed the entire crew out of her office. "And erase that last part!" She yelled before slamming the door in their face.

"Now back to you. Ain't nobody forget nothin'. You just come up in here and spring this shit on me. You didn't even ask me how I might feel. Have you even thought about the kids? How do you think Kiyan and Mila are going to feel about this? It's already bad enough we haven't been gettin' along." She lowered her voice.

"Now you want yo' daddy to come live with us? I don't think you thought this all the way through. You're barely at home as it is. Every other week you're out of town doing God knows what. Who's going to be there with him, 'cause I'm not?"

"Actually, I've been thinkin' about this for months. And look, I understand how you feel but it'll only be for a

minute. I'ma get him his own spot. Just trust me on this."
Black lovingly kissed the side of her face.

Inhaling deeply, Meesa closed her eyes and said
"Okay, but only for a little while."

"Thanks, ma, I knew you would understand." Black
hugged her.

"Yeah, a'ight, we'll see," Meesa sighed not hugging
him back.

"What time you leaving tonight? Let's go out and
have a drink."

"No, Black. I don't wanna go out. Do you ever
think about anything besides kickin' it? Damn," she
remarked with an attitude.

"You don't wanna do shit." Black ice grilled her.

"Some of us have work to do." She pulled away
from his embrace.

"Man, whateva." Black paused for a second.

It was taking everything in him not to reach out and
choke the shit outta her.

"I got something else I need to tell you." He
announced nervously.

"What now, Black?" Meesa took another deep
breath.

Noticing the look of dread in her eyes, Black decided he'd include her in on the rest of his news at a later time. She was already overwhelmed with work, the kids and now the news of his father coming to live with them. Anything else would send her over the edge and the news Black had in store for Meesa was surely going to rock their lives to the core.

SIT IT ON HIS FACE,
WHILE HE HIGH. MAKE
HIS FACE ERASE.
-CHRISS ZOE,
"CONCRETE"

CHAPTER 3

Gwyn sat quietly in the back of Colicchio & Sons, a new, popular New York restaurant, tapping her foot. Every other minute she would check her watch to make sure the time was right. Cash was more than twenty minutes late. *How dare this muthafucka have me picked up from my job to have lunch with him and then have me sitting here like a damn fool?,* Gwyn thought heated. *His ass got five more minutes and I'm up.* She knew Cash ass was full of shit. That's why she never dated men that looked as good as she did or thugs. A good looking brotha felt as if they were God's gift to women and thugs felt like the whole world revolved around them.

Cash was both, so he already had two strikes against him. He had the possibility to sweep Gwyn off of her feet and charm her with his swagger and she wasn't having it. *No more thugs. From now on I'm only dealing with square brothas,* is what she told herself after Trey. Ever since he broke her heart and left her for Lauren London, Gwyn vowed to never give her heart to a man again.

A square brotha was more her speed. Square brothas were reliable and easy to control. They had benefits and shit. 401k's, health insurance, and good credit. They weren't living at home wit' they mama or out moving dope at all times of the night. Nah, a square brotha was out getting his higher education and investing in the stock market.

A square brotha is what Gwyn needed and as of recently, she had convinced herself of that. Staying true to her word, she even went out on a date with a couple. They treated her like gold. She was wined and dined, they said all the right things and took her to all the right places but the spark just wasn't there. Nothing she ever said or did was wrong. Gwyn was always right. Even when she got smart they wouldn't put her in check and on top of that- the conversation was boring as hell. After her fifth date with a square dude, Gwyn looked herself in the mirror and said, *"Fuck it. I change my mind. I need a soldier."* And a solider is just what she got when she met Cash.

Unbeknownst to Cash, his five minutes were almost up when he walked through the doors of the restaurant. He could tell that she was mad as hell as he approached the table. To say that Gwyn was mad was an understatement. She was pissed.

"What's up, beautiful? Sorry I'm late but traffic was a muthafucka." He tried greeting her with a hug.

"Look, you can save that bullshit for the next chick." She dodged his hug. "'Cause I ain't even tryin' to hear it." Gwyn shot getting up from her seat.

"Come on, beautiful, don't leave. I said I was sorry." Cash took her hand and looked into her eyes.

Immediately, a jolt of electricity ran through Gwyn's veins. Cash's hands were as soft as a baby's bottom. His gear wasn't that bad either. He was donned in a Yankee cap, white tee-shirt, Cavalli jeans and Tim's. He didn't have on too much jewelry either. He simply wore an Audemars Piguet watch that cost well over three hundred thousand dollars. Gwyn liked his style, not too many dudes were up on their watch game.

"Don't leave, I'm sorry. I promise I'll make it up to you." He said giving her his saddest puppy dog eyes.

Falling for it hook, line and sinker, Gwyn sat back down. As she did, Cash caught a glimpse of her voluptuous hips and thighs. Gwyn was turning him on to the fullest. She looked just as good as she did at his album release party. She too was dressed casually in a beaded Rachel Roy tunic top, fitted jeans and heels. Her hair was straight with Chinese bangs. Just the sight of her made his dick hard. She looked so good Cash had to adjust his dick as he sat down.

"I forgive you but don't ever have me waiting again," she quipped.

"Oh, so, I get the privilege of seeing you again?"

"Don't get ahead of yourself. I didn't say all that," Gwyn gave him a quick smile.

"To be honest wit' you, I'm surprised you even showed up."

"Why, because you were an arrogant asshole when I met you?" She said simply.

"Well, I wouldn't put it like that but yeah." Cash laughed some.

"You should be ashamed of yourself. I know yo' mama raised you better than that."

"She did and that's why I apologize. What I was trying to say when I met you was that I think you're fly. You bad, ma, and you know it. I like that. Plus the fact that you don't take no shit off of me is a plus."

"I don't take shit off of nobody, especially no man."

"I feel you. So what's going on with you Miss Gwyneth Lee Vice President of Marketing and Promotions for Miss A," Cash teased.

"You got jokes, huh," Gwyn smiled, rolling her eyes. "Life's good. I've just been working that's all. I've been trying to get tickets to go see Adrian Marcel at the Hammerstein Ballroom but they're all sold out."

"What you know about Adrian Marcel?"

"I love him. He's like, one of my favorite artist out right now."

"Besides me of course," Cash flashed a perfect set of teeth.

"You a'ight," Gwyn couldn't help but laugh. "What you been up to?"

"Man, the last few weeks have been crazy. I've been from state to state promoting my new album. If you only knew how tired I am." He said wearily.

"Trust me; I can understand. I work nonstop at my job."

"Straight?"

"Yeah, I mean I love my job don't get me wrong but sometimes it can be very stressful. I guess I don't have too much to complain about though. This job compared to my old one is like a walk in the park." Gwyn examined the menu.

"Why you say that? What you use to do?"

"I used to dance." Gwyn replied, with complete confidence.

"For real? You used to strip?" Cash said surprised.

"Excuse me, I used to dance not strip." Gwyn corrected him.

"My bad. Where?" Cash chuckled, taking a gulp of lemon water.

"Well, I was a feature dancer so I danced at a lot of different clubs."

"Like where?"

"Uhmm…Scores…Larry Flynt…Magic City—"

"Yo, I knew I knew you from somewhere!" Cash interrupted, cutting her off. "What was your stage name? Hallow… Heather—"

"Heroine," Gwyn responded.

"I knew I seen that ass before?" Cash slapped his hand on the table, startling her. "Yo, you don't remember me?" Cash asked shocked.

"Noooo." Gwyn shook her head confused.

"1999… mansion party out in Buckhead?" Cash referred to Buckhead, Atlanta, Georgia.

Gwyn still didn't know what he was talking about.

"Me, you, hot tub, a few ecstasy pills? I was celebrating the success of my mixtape… I went by the name GQ back then."

Suddenly the memories of her past came flooding back; everything from them popping pills to him fucking the shit outta her in the hot tub. It took her a minute because his hair was different and they both were a lot younger. Back then, he wasn't rocking a low cut and he didn't have any tattoos.

Gwyn had completely blocked that part of her life from her memory bank. That night had become the worst night of her life. After they hooked up Gwyn never heard from Cash again. It didn't bother her at first. She'd had plenty of one-night stands. Hell, she didn't even take the time to figure out his real name. The only thing she was concerned with was getting money.

Cash blessed her with a stack and her job was complete. Gwyn never caught feelings for the men she slept with. To her, Cash was just another satisfied customer. It was all good until a few months later when she found out she was pregnant. Gwyn was eighteen, scared and not ready for motherhood.

She wasn't willing to give up her lifestyle either. She loved the rush of getting fast money from stripping.

She had no plans of quitting. There was no way she was going to raise a child in that environment. Gwyn didn't want to abort her baby, so she did the next thing possible. She put the baby up for adoption. She never imagined she'd see Cash again. But here they were sitting inches away from one another. Petrified beyond belief, she grabbed her purse and got up.

"Where you going?" Cash grabbed her hand.

"Look, we might as well end this right now 'cause I'm not like that anymore." Gwyn said at once.

"It's cool, ma, that was the past."

"Nah, Cash, a lot of stuff went down that night." She said, thinking of their baby.

"I'm saying, we were two consensual adults enjoying ourselves. Don't spoil the moment. Damn... I can't believe after all these years I'm seeing you again."

"I know; me too." Gwyn sighed in disbelief as she sat back down.

Something told me to stay my black ass at work, she thought.

"Yo, that night was crazy."

"You got that right. Look, I got something I need to tell you—"

"Whatever you about to say, save it." Cash said, cutting her off. "Like you said, that shit was in the past. You say you ain't the same no more so don't even trip. The only person that can judge you is God."

"Right but—"

"But nothing. Let's order. I'm hungrier than a muthafucka."

TIME TO BACK UP ALL
OF THAT MOUTH
THAT YOU HAD ALL IN
THE CAR.
-BEYONCÉ FEAT. JAY-Z,
"DRUNK IN LOVE"

CHAPTER 4

Every Saturday since moving to New York, Nikki would stay at home watching movies and pigging out. She didn't really like going out by herself, so if the girls didn't go out, neither did she. The building in which she lived had a grocery store, Redbox, edible couture bakery, and laundromat on the same street so she really didn't have any reason to venture outside of her neighborhood.

Slipping her favorite tee-shirt on over her head, she sat on the edge of her four-post, king size bed and placed her favorite house shoes on. Once she was finished, she made her way into her bathroom and brushed her shoulder length, honey blonde hair into a wrap. Securing it with two bobby pins, she then wrapped a paisley silk scarf around her head. Catching her reflection in the mirror, Nikki studied her face for a minute.

She was quietly beautiful. Her skin was fair and as smooth as butter. Men always told her that it looked good enough to eat because her skin was so creamy. She stood five feet, six inches tall and had a very tight, athletic frame.

Nikki made sure to workout at least four to five times a week. Even though she was toned, her body was still very feminine and soft. Her breasts weren't really that big though. They rounded out to be a size 36 B but what her breasts lacked - her ass made up for.

Nikki had what most dudes called a ghetto booty. It wasn't as big as Serena Williams' but if in a competition, she would most definitely come in second. Turning her head from left to right, she admired her brown, doe-shaped eyes and freckles. Her nose was cute and tiny just like a reindeer's but her pink lips were plump and succulent to say the least. Sighting a small bump appearing on her nose, she quickly grabbed a tube of Colgate toothpaste and squirted some onto the tip of her index finger.

After dabbing the toothpaste onto the bump, she rinsed her hands, smiled and headed to the kitchen. Frank Ocean's *Thinkin' about You* was playing in the background as she searched her pantry for a can of smoked oysters and Doritos. Finding them, she snatched a fruit punch Mistic from the fridge, turned off the stereo and went into her sitting room. One of her favorite movies, *Every Girl Should Be Married,* was already on the screen and ready to be viewed.

Making herself comfortable on the couch, she pressed play. Twenty minutes into the movie and almost done with her oyster and Dorito combination, she heard her cell phone ring. Placing her one-of-a-kind snack down, Nikki raced into the kitchen to answer it.

"Hello?"

"What up, baby girl?"

A smile instantly formed on her face. It was OJ.

"Hi," she spoke sweetly.

"What you up to?"

"Nothing, watching a movie," she blushed.

So far Nikki and OJ's phone conversations had been going well. The only problem was that they barely had time to talk and hadn't seen each other since the album release party. OJ had been busy on Cash's promotional tour and she'd been busy preparing for Fashion Week.

"Oh, so you just gon' watch a movie without me?" He teased.

"Yep," she giggled.

"That's fucked up." He laughed too. "I can't get no love?"

"You know if you were in town I would've invited you over."

"Is that right?" He spoke low into the phone.

"Mmm hmm."

"Come open the door then."

"What?" Nikki replied, nervously looking around the room.

"Open the door."

"You're here for real?" Her heart pounded out of her chest.

"Yeah," he insisted.

As she walked anxiously towards the door, Nikki wondered if he was really in the hallway or was he just fucking with her. Once she looked out the peephole and saw that he was really there, she damn near shitted on herself.

"Damn, what took you so long?" OJ asked as she opened the door.

"I didn't think you were really here." Nikki said, barely able to breathe.

"I wanted to kick it wit' you tonight so I decided to swing through."

"How did you even no where I lived?" She asked, still holding the phone in her hand confused.

"First, hang up the phone," OJ chuckled.

"Oh shit, my bad." Nikki clicked the phone off.

"Your homegirl Gwyn told me."

"I'ma kick her ass."

"Can I come in or not?" OJ probed.

"My bad, yeah, sure." Nikki stepped to the side to let him in.

Catching a whiff of the smoked oysters, OJ covered his nose with his hand and asked, "Did I catch you at a bad time?"

"Oh my God!" Nikki hollered, embarrassed.

Beet red, she ran over to the coffee table and retrieved her unusual snack.

"It's cool, ma," he laughed. "My ole dude used to eat sardines and pigs feet."

"I am so embarrassed," Nikki giggled nervously.

After dumping the oysters into the trash can, she sprayed the house profusely with Glade air freshener.

"So, what you been up to? I ain't talk to you in a minute." OJ sat down on the edge of the couch.

"You act like that's my fault. You the one who hasn't called me," she replied, with a hint of sarcasm in her voice.

"Here you go. You know I'm on the road for like a month straight sometimes, doing shows. I was gon' call you but a nigga was tied up."

"Yeah, yeah." Nikki waved him off as she sat next to him on the couch.

"I'm for real. I was gon' get at you." OJ looked at her out of the corner of his eye.

"Mmm hmm, that's what your mouth say."

"I see now you one of them chicks that don't believe nothin' a nigga say."

"You got that right. Y'all dudes lie too much."

"Well, I ain't one of them brothas, so you ain't got to worry about me lying to you. But anyway, enough of that. Why don't you go in the back and put on something sexy? I wanna take you out."

"Take me out where?" Nikki said surprised.

"To this club. One of my pot'nahs is having a party there tonight. I told him I'd swing through."

"Do you see me right now? I look a hot mess." Nikki looked down at her outfit.

"Yeah, I meant to ask you. What's up wit' the toothpaste on your nose?" OJ pointed at her nose.

Nikki couldn't have been more embarrassed.

"I was getting a bump on my nose so I put it on there so it would go away." She quickly covered up her nose.

"Come here." OJ patted his thigh.

Doing as she was asked, Nikki stood up and eased down onto his lap.

"Take your hand off your face."

Nikki reluctantly did as she was told.

"Don't ever be ashamed of anything around me. Okay?" He tickled her stomach.

"Ok." Nikki giggled uncontrollably.

"Ok?" OJ licked the toothpaste off her nose.

"Ok-ok-ok!" She laughed hysterically.

"Now go get dressed. I wanna show you off tonight."

Meesa and Black entered their bedroom after putting their kids to bed. Meesa absolutely adored her bedroom. She'd spent months decorating it and once finished, was rewarded with a feature on elledécor.com. The staff at Elle loved her mixture of masculine and feminine pieces. The entire room was black and white. In the center of the room was a huge king size bed with an abundance of black and white pillows on top.

A gorgeous black and white dresser sat against the wall next to a black dress design mannequin. To finish off the room was a white leather couch, plush, zebra print rug, mirrored nightstands and black and white photos of Meesa, Black and their children. The only drawback to the room was sharing it with her husband.

Ever since Black dropped the bomb on her that his father would be staying with them, things between the two were even more strained. Whenever Meesa tried to spark up a conversation, Black always seemed preoccupied. Every time she turned around, he was either texting or having secret conversations on his phone.

Meesa tried her best to go on with her daily life as if nothing was wrong but the nagging suspicion that Black was back to no good kept eating at her. She didn't want to admit it to anyone, not even herself, that he could be cheating on her again but the evidence was right in her face. She just didn't know if this time she would be able to physically or mentally handle the truth once it finally hit the surface.

"So how was your day?" Meesa asked, placing on her pajamas.

"It was cool." Black turned his back to her and sat down on the bed.

"Okay," Meesa scoffed. "How was your day, Meesa?" She asked herself. "Oh it was fine. Thanks for asking."

Not in the mood to argue, Black ignored her and got underneath the covers.

"Oh word? That's how you feel? Like really, Black? You just gon' sit there and ignore me?" Meesa snapped, feeling her temperature rise.

"I'm not gettin' ready to argue wit' you tonight. We both got a lot of shit going on. So why don't you just lie down and go to bed." Black replied, trying his best to remain calm.

He knew that his wife was at her breaking point but all would reveal itself in due time.

Meesa clenched her jaw and shook her head.

"A'ight." She got into bed.

"Goodnight." Black rested his head on his pillow.

"Just tell me. Are you mad at me or something? Did I do something to you?" Meesa said, unable to let the situation go.

"No, I'm just tired, that's all. Let it go."

Meesa wished that she could believe him but they'd been together far too long for her not to know when something was wrong with her husband. Black just wasn't himself anymore and Meesa didn't know how to fix him or her marriage. Sick of stressing over him, Meesa decided a good night's sleep would do her and him some good. But halfway through the night as she and Black slept on opposite sides of the bed, the telephone rang startling them both. Alarmed and disoriented, Meesa reached out and picked up the phone.

"Hello," she answered groggily.

"MEESA!"

"Mina?" Meesa turned on the light and sat up. "What's wrong? It's not daddy is it?"

"No! It's Victor! He just called and said that he had to lay low for a minute!" Mina cried hysterically. "Meesa, he's gone and he's not coming back!"

"Damn," Meesa soaked in the information. "Okay just calm down."

"I don't know what to do. The only thing Victor said was call Black and then he hung up."

"Why would he tell you to call Black?" Meesa asked, confused.

"Let me talk to her." Black took the phone away from her ear.

"Mina, listen." Black spoke in a calming tone. "Everything gon' be straight. Me and Meesa gon' be on the first flight out there tonight. I'll fill you in on everything once we get there."

"Okay," Mina replied, wiping her nose.

"And don't call anybody and say shit. Just sit tight; we'll be there as soon as we can."

"Okay," Mina replied, getting off of the phone.

"Here." Black ended the call and handed Meesa back her phone. "Get dressed."

"What was that all about?" She eyed him suspiciously.

Black licked his bottom lip and inhaled deeply. For months this was the moment he'd prepared for but now that it was here he wasn't ready. What he had to tell his wife would change things between them forever and not for the better. He was done with playing Mr. Mom and attending industry events. It was time for him to get back to the core of who he was.

With Victor underground and no one else in the Gonzales family to take over, Black would hold the crown. He was already certain that Meesa would go off and have a fit but this was the decision he'd made. She'd either ride it out with him or... Black didn't even wanna think about losing Meesa. She was his everything but he had to do this for Victor and for himself.

Meesa sat across from Black with her legs crossed, angry as hell. It was the crack of dawn and they were on a private plane heading to St. Louis. Black refused to tell her anything until they got to Mina's house. Meesa hated being in the dark. It was obvious that he had been keeping things from her. They used to tell each other everything. Somewhere communication between them broke down and now here they were.

Meesa felt like they were practically strangers. For the last few years they'd been drifting apart. The more her career and fame rose, the more Black pulled away. He hated the limelight. He was a hood nigga to the heart. He didn't like the paparazzi and tabloids all up in their business. Meesa acted like his name didn't use to once ring bells in the streets. It was only a matter of time before the world knew that her husband was a former drug dealer and stone cold killer.

They'd been faking that he was a business man for so long that she'd started to believe her own lies. Black was done pretending that he was happy with the way their life was. He loved his wife and kids but the itch to get back in the game was driving him insane. He had to remind Meesa, the streets and more importantly himself exactly who the fuck he was. As soon as they landed in St. Louis there was a Rolls-Royce Phantom awaiting their arrival.

Mina sent over her driver, Paul, to pick them up. Meesa stepped off the plane looking like she'd had hours to plan her look when really she only had minutes to get dressed. She looked like a bag of money in a $154 Riller & Fount white, scoop neck, pocket tee, skin tight, white, skinny leg jeans and black Christian Louboutin Pigalle heels. A pair of black Ray-Ban wafer shades covered her eyes. A silver tribal inspired statement necklace and black Celine bag finished her look. Black followed behind her looking dapper as well. He rocked an Obey floral print sweatshirt, Hermès belt, distressed fitted jeans, gold, Rolex watch and Tim's.

Meesa and Black got into the back of the Phantom and continued to sit in silence. Meesa looked out the window. Her kids were on her mind. It was time for them to go to school and she wasn't there. She was always there to see them off to school. But no, here she was in St. Louis. Everything that was fucked up in her life happened in St. Louis. She'd lost her mother, her best friend and was almost murdered herself there.

The only good thing to come out of St. Louis was her meeting and falling in love with Black and even now that wasn't good. Meesa couldn't wait to get back to New York. St. Louis was a death trap. Only killers, opportunist, hoes, liars, pretenders, wannabes and thieves roamed those streets. She wanted no parts of it.

"How long are we going to be here?" Meesa asked Black as they passed up what used to be Northwest Plaza.

The old mall was now a knocked down pile of rubble.

"A day or two," he replied not even bothering to look up from his phone.

"Let's make it a day. I want to get back to my kids."

"Keep it one hundred." Black looked at her. "You wanna get back to your job."

"Yeah, I do and? I was supposed to film today but I had to cancel because you're on some secretive bullshit."

"I told you that all would reveal itself in due time."

"Okay, David Copperfield." Meesa waved him off. "Ain't nobody got time for this hocus pocus bullshit you on."

"You really need to fix your fuckin' attitude. Your mouth has gotten real reckless here lately. Don't act like I won't fuck you up." Black mean mugged her.

"I don't need to fix shit." Meesa rolled her neck.

"Yeah you do. I don't know who the fuck you think I am. You better watch your fuckin' mouth," Black warned.

"I know you ain't talkin' to me," Meesa scoffed, looking around the backseat of the car in disbelief.

"Who the fuck else am I talkin' to?"

"Obviously not me 'cause a nigga with the name *Latrell* can't tell me shit," Meesa shot.

She knew that Black hated his government name.

"Now you tryin' to be funny." Black clenched his jaw. "Keep it up and I'ma fuck you up."

"Fuck me up," Meesa challenged. "You the man. Shut me up." She took off her shades and stared him directly in the eye.

Black looked at Meesa and grinned. He knew his wife like he knew the back of his hand. She wanted some dick and she wanted it bad. He and Meesa argued like cats and dogs but one thing that hadn't changed about them was their sexual attraction for one another. When they did have sex it was always earth-shattering. She stayed on his dick and that's how Black liked it. Nothing pleased him more than to hear his wife moan and scream out his name.

Black pressed the button to raise the partition. Meesa bit into her bottom lip and unzipped her jeans.

Seconds later they were off. She wore no panties. Black got onto his knees and parted her legs. Meesa looked at his face.

"You gon' learn to shut the fuck up." Black ice grilled her before burying his face in-between her thighs.

"Shut up." Meesa gasped for air then threw her legs over his shoulders.

"Ahhhhh! Mmmmmm...baby!"

Black sucked on her clit with no remorse. He had to teach Meesa a lesson. She had to stop treating him like he was a sucker. She knew how he got down. She liked it when the hood side of him came out but only in the bedroom. What Meesa didn't understand was that there was no taming a beast. Black wasn't to be fucked with. Each stroke of his tongue on her clit proved it. Meesa ran her hands threw his locs and squeezed her eyes tight. Black had begun thumbing her clit.

"Shit! Ahhhhh, baby."

Black came up for air and stared at Meesa's pussy hungrily. She had the prettiest pussy he'd ever seen. He loved feasting on her pink kitty.

"You like that shit don't you?" Meesa panted.

"Shut up and sit on my dick." Black sat down and pulled out his brown, thick dick.

It was rock hard and standing at full attention. Meesa climbed on top of him and eased down slowly on his dick. They were ten years into their relationship and she still hadn't gotten use to his length and girth.

"Ride daddy dick!" Black slapped her ass cheek. "We almost there."

Meesa bounced up and down on Black's dick while he palmed her ass. Her juices were streaming down his dick like a waterfall. The sound of her moans and her juices slapping against his shaft filled the car. Neither of them cared that the driver might be able to hear them. They were lost in one another.

"Mmmmmm, baby, you feel so good. I needed this."

"I know you did." Black cupped the back of her head and bit into her neck.

No other chick could compare to her. She was the shit. After two kids her body was still tight and there wasn't a stretch mark on her. Her body was a wonderland and Black wanted to spend the rest of his life exploring every crevice of it. He could never get enough of her. She was his world.

"Tell me you love me." He demanded, pumping his dick in and out of her at a feverish pace.

"I love you." Meesa placed her forehead on his. She could feel herself about to cum.

"Ahhhhhhhhh! Black! Shit!" She screeched.

Tears were forming in her eyes - his dick felt so good. No other man on Earth could make her feel the way Black did. She'd take her last breath lying by his side. That was how God intended. They'd been through the storm together. They'd get through this little rough patch too. Black and Meesa had a forever kind of love. Nothing could break them up.

"Baby, I love you." Meesa locked eyes with her husband.

"I love you too," Black groaned.

"Shit, I love you," Meesa shrilled. "I love you-I love you-I love you," she climaxed.

After coming down from their orgasmic high, Black and Meesa put their clothes back on. They'd pulled up to Mina's compound. Meesa was always taken aback about how massive the estate was. Mina's $63 million, 20 acre compound had seven bedrooms, 18 bathrooms, a media screening and projection room, 2 elevators and a 17 car garage.

"You ready?" Black asked, straightening his clothes.

Meesa examined her face in her Dior compact mirror. Her face was a little moist from their sexcapade but other than that she looked perfect.

"Yeah." She put the mirror back inside her purse.

Black stepped out of the car first then reached back for Meesa's hand. Paul got their bags out of the trunk. Black and Meesa didn't even get a chance to knock on the door before it flew open.

"Thank God you're here!" Mina cried out tears of joy.

Seeing her sister always freaked Mina out. They could've been twins. The only difference between them was Mina's hair was long and black and she was a size 16. She was beautiful nonetheless.

"Sister!" Meesa rushed into Mina's awaiting arms.

"I missed you." Mina squeezed her tight.

"Not more than I missed you."

"Can I get in on this hug?" Black joked.

"I'm sorry, Black," Mina giggled. "How are you?" She hugged him.

"I'm good. The question is, how are you?"

"I'ma wreck. Can't you tell? Come on in." She stepped to the side.

Meesa and Black stepped into Mina's foyer and looked around in awe. Mina's foyer shitted on their entire penthouse apartment in New York. Meesa never asked her sister but word on the street was that Victor was worth over 700 million dollars. It made perfect sense that the feds would be on his ass.

"Where are my niece and nephew? Meesa asked as Mina led them into one of the living rooms.

"They're at school. You'll get to see them this afternoon. How are Kiyan and Mila?"

"Bad as fuck," Black joked.

"No they're not." Meesa playfully hit Black on the arm. "They're good. When all of this chaos dies down you're going to have to come up and see them."

"Speaking of chaos." Mina sat down on the couch. "Let's get down to business. What is going on, Black? I'm losing my freakin' mind."

Before Black replied, he sat quietly as the maid brought in a tray of coffee, tea, croissants, cream cheese, salmon and other delicious breakfast treats.

"Can I get you anything else, ma'am?" The maid asked.

"No, thank you." Mina shook her head.

The maid left the room.

"Black, you have to tell me what's going on? I haven't slept all night. Where is my husband?" Mina wiped her nose with a tissue.

"Victor is straight. He's somewhere safe."

"Why wouldn't he tell me that he was leaving? I mean he just up and left. The only thing I have is this punk-ass note saying I love you and I'll be gone for a while. I even have instructions to burn it."

"Yeah, give me that." Black took the note from Mina's hand and burned it with a lighter.

He quickly threw it in the fire place and watched it burn.

"He didn't tell you where he was going because if you're brought in for questioning he wants you to honestly not know a thing. I'm the only person that knows where he's at and even I don't know the exact location. That's how careful we're being."

"But why? What is going on?"

"The feds have been building a case against Victor for a few years now. A lot of people have gotten knocked and started snitching. They've been throwing out Victor's name. The feds don't have any concrete evidence on Victor or an I.D yet but they're close. Before things got too hot,

Victor felt it was best to dip for a while until things cool down. That's where I come in at."

"What do you mean?" Meesa asked confused.

Black looked over at his wife. He swallowed hard. This was the moment he'd been dreading and eagerly awaiting for months.

"While Victor's gone he wants me to oversee things," he confessed.

"Excuse me?" Meesa shook her head, praying she hadn't heard right. "What did you say?"

"We've been planning this for months now. In Victor's absence I'm going to take over and make sure that business is running smooth, like always. I'll be making regular trips to St. Louis to check the books and so forth."

"Oh no the hell you're not." Meesa shot up from her seat. "Have you lost your fuckin' mind? I'm not doing this shit with you again. And secondly, how are you going to make this decision without me? You rappin' with Victor like he's your fuckin' wife."

"Pause." Black held up his hand. "You going too far."

"No, you are! I'm not down with this. When we left St. Louis you left that shit behind you, remember? You promised me that you were done with that shit for good."

"I know what I said but Victor needs my help and honestly I need to do this for myself. I'm sorry you're upset but I'm doing this with or without you. So you just gon' have to deal with it."

"Oh word?" Meesa scoffed drawing her head back. "That's how you feel?"

"Yeah." Black glared back at her not backing down.

"Ok…. then know that from this day moving forward you gon' be doing a lot of shit without me. You're on your own, bruh." Meesa spat, storming off.

I KNOW THAT'S YO'
MAN. HE AIN'T GOT
NO BANDS THOUGH.
-TINY FEAT. SHEKINAH,
"CUT IT OFF"

CHAPTER 5

Meesa had an hour before it was time to board the plane back to New York but she had to visit her mother's grave. She'd feel like an absolute shithead if she didn't. Whenever she did visit home, which was rarely, she always made it her business to stop by and talk to her mom. Black was back at Mina's packing his things. Meesa told him that she wanted to come alone.

Plus, things between them were so shaky that she didn't feel like getting into another argument with him. After his bombshell, Meesa was emotionally wrecked. She was so angry with Black that she couldn't even bear looking at his face. Meesa walked slowly towards her mother's grave with a bouquet of yellow roses in hand. Her heart was beating a mile a minute.

The mere thought of death freaked her out, so to be at her mother's grave terrified her. Meesa liked to pretend that her mother was on a long vacation. It still wasn't real to her that she was gone. She missed her tremendously. Meesa stood in front of her mother's tombstone. The flowers she'd left years before had almost deteriorated. Meesa grabbed what was left of the stems and threw them to the side. She placed the new flowers inside of the holder and smiled. Her mother loved yellow roses. They were her favorite.

"Hey, mama."

Meesa looked down at her name that was engraved in the tombstone.

"Sorry it's been so long but you know I hate coming here. Coming here makes it so real."

Meesa looked around at all the other graves.

"I wish you could see the kids. They're so big, mama. Kiyan is almost taller than me now and he's so handsome. He looks just like his father. Oh and Mila... Mila is something else," Meesa laughed.

"That girl has a mouth on her but she's so beautiful. She reminds me a lot of you. She's fearless, mama, and sometimes that scares me 'cause I want to shield her from everything bad in the world. But she's growing into her own little person so I guess I have to let her be. I just don't know, ma."

Tears filled Meesa's eyes.

"Everything in my life is just moving so fast and I can't keep up. I mean this is what I always wanted but now that I have it I sometimes wonder if it's all worth it. It seemed like life was so much easier when I lived in my one bedroom apartment. At least then I had my sanity."

Tears dripped down Meesa's face.

"Mama, my marriage is falling apart and I don't know how to fix it. The kids hear us fighting all the time. We fight over the dumbest shit. Everything I say or do gets on his nerves. He doesn't show any emotion outside of anger and lust. He's unhappy and nothing that I say or do makes it better. Now I find out he's been keeping secrets from me. I don't know what to do. Every day I feel him slipping further and further away from me. We've been faking being happy for the last few years and I can't tell my friends 'cause to them we're the picture-perfect couple. I just want my old life back, mama," Meesa sobbed.

"I want things to go back to the way they used to be. I would give it all up if I had you and my husband back. But you're gone and I feel like he's leaving me too, especially now that he's decided to get back into the game. I understand that he's trying to help my sister and her husband out but nothing good is gonna come from this. I can feel it."

"Mrs. Patterson," Paul said. "Sorry to interrupt but it's time to head to the airport."

"Ok." Meesa wiped her face with the back of her hand.

She looked back down at her mother's grave with sorrow.

"Mama, I need your help. Please watch over us. We're gonna need all the help we can get."

With Meesa out of the office on an unexpected business trip and Gwyn taking a so-called sick day, that left Kelly in charge of everything. She was swamped with work and in charge of the whole entire company in their absence. Kelly loved the challenge but running a billion dollar company and having the stresses of dealing wit' a nigga at home that didn't want to do shit with his life was deeming too difficult to handle.

Any day or moment Kelly was going to explode. Work and Jaden were both driving her insane. Something was going to have to give and soon. Hell, she was the one who needed a sick day. It had been years since she took a vacation. Kelly couldn't afford to take time off. She had her son and a grown-ass man to take care of. It cost money to live the way they did. They'd been living lavishly since back in St. Louis when Jaden was the bread winner.

Kelly never had to want for nothing. He kept her laced in the hottest gear. She stayed pushing expensive whips and she never left the house without dripping in diamonds. At first Kelly was cool with holding down the family. Jaden had taken care of her for years. It was only right she returned the favor when he fell off but nothing was more unattractive than being the man in the relationship.

Kelly felt like she was the man and Jaden was her bitch. She paid for everything: their house, cars, clothes and food. She even paid when they went out on dates. It was like she was dating herself. The shit wasn't cute. She wanted to feel like she was secure and safe. She hated having to rely on herself when she had a grown-ass man lying next to her at night. Nothing about her and Jaden's relationship was right.

Somewhere he lost his confidence and drive. Kelly loved him with all of her heart but she didn't have the time or the energy to be raising somebody else's son. She had a son of her own to raise. Jaden had to step up and become his own encouragement. She was over being his cheerleader. It was time for him to either ship up or shape out. Kelly turned to her computer and pulled up the sales chart for the month when her male assistant, Tyler, knocked lightly on the door.

"Excuse me, Kelly, but you have a visitor."

"Who is it?" Kelly asked curious as to who it might be.

"He says his name is Dre and girl he is hot," Tyler mouthed.

Kelly's heart instantly stopped beating and her palms began to sweat. *What in the hell is he doing here,* she thought. Kelly quickly glanced in the mirror on her desk. She was on point. Her locs were pulled up in a bun. She wore very little makeup just some mascara and a matte, plum lipstick that accentuated her full lips. She rocked a chic, white, asymmetrical hemmed blazer, a white button up that was unbuttoned halfway and tucked inside a pair of white shorts. On her feet was a pair of sickening, metallic silver, 6 inch, YSL pointed toe pumps.

"Send him in," she said confidently.

Dre glided into her office as if he were walking on air. Kelly swallowed hard and tried her damnest to hide her excitement. Dre was fine as fuck. His swag was on a hundred. He and the rapper Nas could've been twins.

As soon as he crossed the threshold of her door, the smell of his Clive Christian X perfume engulfed her nostrils. She was immediately hypnotized. His laid-back sex appeal turned her on to the fullest. Dre rocked a simple, black, Stefani Ricci dress shirt. The top four buttons were undone, exposing his firm, tattooed chest and a thin, gold rosary. The rest of his look consisted of black Saint Laurent jeans, black, leather Lanvin dress shoes and a Gucci boule bracelet.

"Hello, stalker." Kelly leaned back in her chair.

"You wish I was a stalker." Dre chuckled sitting down across from her.

"If you're looking for Meesa or Destiny they're not here."

"Actually, I came to see you."

"What can I do for you?" Kelly crossed her legs.

Dre admired her long, lean legs. He wondered how they would feel wrapped around his back.

"I was in the area and decided to come check you out, Miss Kelly." He picked up one of her business cards.

"Ok, you see me; now you can leave." She shooed him away

"Why you so mean? You're way too pretty to be so fuckin' mean."

"I'm not mean. I'm busy… and I don't have time for a bunch of games. Now if you'll excuse me, I have work to get back to."

"Work? Have you looked outside today? It's beautiful. Come spend the day with me. We can go have lunch. Catch a Broadway show, anything you like," Dre smiled.

His raspy voice was like music to Kelly's ears.

"I'm good," Kelly cocked her head to the side. "And besides… I don't think my man would like that."

Dre leaned closer.

"I don't see no ring on your finger."

"And what that mean?" Kelly arched her brow.

"It means that nigga ain't shit but your boyfriend. He ain't nothing but a boy that's your friend. You don't owe him shit. Be an adult. Have an affair for once." Dre shot her a devilish grin.

Kelly couldn't help but grin.

"Your little speech was cute. I liked it… but no. I love my man and I'm faithful to my man. I'm pretty sure there are plenty of eligible, single women in New York City that would love to spend the day with you."

"But none of those single, eligible women are as pretty as you."

"The answer is still no," Kelly laughed.

"You sure?"

"Very," Kelly confirmed.

"Okay." Dre shrugged his shoulders and stood up.

"Let me know when you get tired of playing house wit' ya' *boy... friend*," he stressed. "Give ya' boy a call when you're ready to fuck wit' a real nigga." He placed his card on her desk, winked his eye and left.

The wind blew through Gwyn's long hair as she drove down the highway. G-Eazy's *Far Alone* played while she gripped the steering wheel with her right hand and ran her fingers through her hair with the left. She could feel her iPhone buzzing on her lap. It was Cash calling her. He'd been calling her since their date but Gwyn hadn't bothered to pick up. Reconnecting with him was the last thing she'd ever expected to happen. She'd completely blocked him from her memory bank.

He was a part of her shady past. She was a different person now. She no longer had to lie, cheat and steal to get ahead. Now she was taken seriously as a business woman. She wasn't ashamed of her past. She was ashamed of some of the fucked up choices she made. The biggest mistake she'd made in her life was giving her baby up for adoption.

During her pregnancy, Gwyn stayed in Atlanta. She didn't even want to know the sex of the baby in fear she'd get too attached. When she finally went into labor and gave birth, Gwyn wasn't even sure if she wanted to hold the baby but when she heard the baby's first cry, her motherly instincts kicked in. She'd tried so hard to be unattached and to not feel a thing but hearing her baby cry reminded her that what was happening was real and not just a figment of her imagination.

She couldn't brush it off like it was nothing. She'd just given birth to a child. A child that after a few minutes, she'd never have claims to again. When the nurse asked her if she'd like to hold the baby, Gwyn had prepared herself to say no but instead her lips parted and she said yes. Tears streamed down her face as the nurse placed her beautiful, healthy baby in her arms. Gwyn's heart melted immediately upon sight but she had to remind herself that giving up her baby for adoption was the best thing for both of them.

Gwyn wasn't mature or stable enough to raise a child. She was constantly on the go. She made her living as an exotic dancer, shaking her ass and titties from state to state. She couldn't raise her baby in that kind of environment. Gwyn needed to get her life together and figure out who she was and what she wanted out of life. Raising a baby would only complicate things, so she kissed the baby on the forehead and gave it back to the nurse.

She had to convince herself that the decision she was making would benefit the both of them. Gwyn would be able to get her life together and her baby would have a normal, peaceful life with a family that would be able to raise her right. After that day Gwyn never looked back. Six weeks later she packed up and left Atlanta. Gwyn was on the first flight back to St. Louis. She went on with her life as if nothing had happened.

Her friends didn't even know about the baby. She'd kept it a secret from them. The only person who knew about the baby was her mother. Now her past was coming back to haunt her. She'd never admit it but she was actually digging Cash. Ever since their date, he'd been on her hard. She tried to resist his advances but his charm and quick wit captivated her. Talking to him was pointless though. He could never know her secret.

Gwyn had to cut off all communication. Cash might be the shit. He might be sexy as fuck and from what she remembered, his dick game was sinfully delicious but none of that mattered. She was done. Their rekindled romance was over before it had even begun. Tired of reminiscing on her fucked up past, Gwyn made her way into Jersey City. She had other things to worry about than Cash.

Her day was going great until she got a call from her little sister Stevie's school. It seemed like every other week Stevie was getting in some type of trouble. That day she was reprimanded for not wearing her uniform in the appropriate way and for refusing to participate and do her work in class. Gwyn didn't know what she was going to do with her. She couldn't afford to leave work every time Stevie got in trouble but somebody had to do it.

Her mother had a bad leg and back so Gwyn had to step up to the plate. Her little sister was heading down a dangerous path. Stevie was so much like Gwyn it scared her. She was fearless, constantly defied authority and had a mouth on her that would shame the devil. It didn't help that at the age of fourteen she was built like a video vixen.

Gwyn had worked her ass off to move her mother and little sister to Jersey. They stayed in a beautiful home in Franklin Lakes. Neither Stevie nor her mother had to want for a thing. Gwyn made sure that they were well taken care of. She paid all of the bills and gave her mother $3,000 a month for spending money. Gwyn even paid for

Stevie to go to the prestigious, private school - Brookfield Academy.

Stevie was given opportunities that Gwyn could only dream of when she was her age. She wasted every one of them though. For some reason she was determined to be this ghetto, hood chick that gave zero fucks. Gwyn pulled up to the front of the school and turned her keys over to the valet. The young valet couldn't take his eyes off Gwyn's derriere as she sauntered up the steps.

Gwyn was serving sex on a stick in a white camisole, skin tight, leopard print, pencil skirt and six inch, red Pigalle Louboutin heels. As soon as Gwyn entered the office she was escorted into the principal's office. Inside she found Principal Moore and Stevie awaiting her arrival. Stevie sat unfazed on her iPhone, popping gum. Gwyn couldn't believe her eyes. Stevie had completely slutted her uniform out.

She took the naughty school girl look to a whole new level. Her white, short sleeve button up was unbuttoned, exposing her black, lace bra and full breasts. The bottom of the shirt was tied into a knot so that her flat, toned stomach could show. Stevie's plaid neck tie was loose and her plaid skirt was cut so short that it almost exposed her vagina. Instead of wearing the required knee high socks, she wore white thigh high stockings with a garter belt and heels.

Like her sister, she was an exotic beauty. Stevie had long, jet black, silky hair, slanted, almond-shaped eyes, button nose and pouty, pink lips. Stevie had gone through puberty at an early age so at the age of fourteen she already had large D cup breasts, hips and a round ass. Men automatically assumed she was an adult but she wasn't. She was Gwyn's baby sister whom she swore to protect. There was no way she was going to sit back and watch her make the same mistakes she had in her younger days.

"Girl... have you lost your damn mind?" Gwyn snapped appalled.

"Hey, sis," Stevie smiled, taking her eyes off her phone for a brief second.

"Hello, Miss Lee." Principal Moore stood up to greet her.

"Hello, Mrs. Moore." Gwyn shook her head. "Before we speak, let me get her together real quick." She turned and faced Stevie who wasn't paying either of them any attention.

"Get off the goddamn phone."

"Hold up, I'm posting this picture on Instagram," Stevie kept on typing.

"Lies you tell." Gwyn snatched Stevie's phone away from her.

"Stop! What you doing?" Stevie whined trying to take it back.

"Fix your uniform," Gwyn ordered.

"Huhhhh; y'all trippin'." Stevie rolled her eyes.

"If I have to tell you one more time it's gon' be on." Gwyn warned.

Stevie knew when her sister wasn't playing. Rolling her eyes, she stood up, untied her shirt and buttoned it up. There was nothing she could do about the barely there skirt.

"Thank you," Gwyn spat.

"Miss Lee, please have a seat." Principal Moore requested.

Gwyn sat down fuming.

"Today in Stevie's math class, Stevie refused to participate. She wouldn't stop talking to her friends and as you can see, she has refused to follow our school uniform policy.

"Your way sucks," Stevie mumbled.

"You better shut up." Gwyn cut her eyes at Stevie.

"I feel that at this point since putting Stevie in in-school and after-school suspension hasn't worked, we here at Brookfield have no choice but to suspend Stevie for three days," Principal Moore confirmed.

"Yes," Stevie fist pumped the air.

"I swear to God I'ma slap you." Gwyn ice grilled her. "I'm sorry, Mrs. Moore. My mother and I will be having a long talk with Stevie. You have my word that after this suspension is over you will no longer have any more problems out of Stevie. Now grab your things. Let's go." She said to Stevie.

Outside the building Gwyn stood with her arms akimbo. She was beyond pissed at Stevie. She couldn't wait for the valet to pull her car around so she could dig in her ass. Seconds later, they were inside the car and heading to their mother's house. Stevie could tell by the pensive expression on her sister's face that she was heated. Stevie hated disappointing her sister but nobody understood the pain she was going through.

"I love you, sister." Stevie wrapped her arms around Gwyn's neck and kissed her on the cheek.

"Girl, bye." Gwyn pushed her away. "Haven't I told you about your fuckin' uniform? All you have to do is go to school and fuckin' learn, that's it. Why is that so hard for you? I'm getting real sick of this shit, Stevie. Why can't you just go to school, do your work and wear your uniform correctly?"

"Umm... have you looked at me? I am serving body, ma'am, and the world needs to see it. What's wrong with that?"

"You're fourteen, li'l girl, that's what's wrong. You have your whole life to show off your body. Trust me; I know."

"You always say that but it's 2014 - times have changed since you were my age," Stevie rolled her eyes.

"I'm for real. I can't keep leaving work early to come all the way to Jersey to deal with you and your bullshit. Can you please act like you got a li'l bit of the sense God and Blue Ivy gave you? I know it's some up there. Let me see." Gwyn pulled Stevie's head over to her so she could examine it.

"Common sense, where are you?"

"Stop, Gwyn! You gon' mess up my hair!" Stevie slapped her hand away.

"It looked like shit anyway."

"Hater," Stevie laughed. "Can we go to the mall?"

"The mall for what?" Gwyn scrunched up her forehead.

"These new Jeremy Scott shoes just came out and I have to get them."

"Uh, no, ma'am." Gwyn focused on the road. "I just took you shopping a few weeks ago and spent a little over two grand on you. Plus, I am no longer rewarding your badass behavior. Get your shit together and then we can talk."

"Whatever," Stevie pulled down the visor mirror and applied a coat of pink glitter lip gloss to her lips.

Stevie was obsessed with her looks. She was the shit and she knew it. Chicks hated her and niggas loved her. She didn't care that her sister told her no about hitting up the mall. All Stevie had to do was hit up one of her boo thangs and they'd take her. Stevie didn't fuck with boys her age.

All of the dudes she messed with were in their twenties. Older dudes loved her sweet, innocent face and curvaceous frame. Why give a fuck about school when she stayed lace in designer labels and dated the finest, flyest dudes in Jersey City? Living the fast life was far more appealing. Stevie was doing her and nothing or no one was going to stop her.

Gwyn parked her car in her mother's driveway and got out. Stevie followed suit as she texted her boo, Wiz. He was down for tearing up the mall and Stevie was willing to lie on her back in exchange for some designer duds. Gwyn used her key and walked inside her mother's home.

"Mama!" Gwyn called out while taking off her heels.

Gwyn's mother didn't want the dirt from outside inside her house.

"I'm in the kitchen!" Regina replied.

"Hi, mama!" Stevie spoke then dashed up the steps to her room.

"What you doing here?" Regina asked as Gwyn came into the kitchen.

Gwyn's mother was a gorgeous black woman. She had the smoothest, bronze colored skin. Her hair was short and dyed honey blonde. Regina's doe-shaped eyes and megawatt smile lit up an entire room. She was a small and petite woman that loved to gamble and cuss. Gwyn didn't know what she would do without her mother. She was a godsend.

Regina raised her girls without the help of either of their father. She worked her butt off for years at GM to take care of her girls. After injuring herself on the job, Regina retired from working on the assembly line and had been living a peaceful life at home ever since. She and Gwyn often butted heads but no matter what, Regina had Gwyn's back.

"I had to go pick up your badass daughter from school. The school called me again about her behavior and uniform. She got suspended this time for three days. Stevie is out of control, mama. She talks back to all her teachers. She's constantly getting into fights when she decides to attend school and her grades are shitty as hell. We gotta do something about this."

"We?" Regina looked at her in disbelief. "We ain't gotta do shit. You mean I have to do something about this. You pop in and say your two cents every few weeks and then disappear back into the city. I'm the one that has to deal with your sister on a day-to-day basis. That's my child and I'm doing the best that I can with her. I'm too old to be whoopin' her. Punishments don't work 'cause she just sneaks out of the house. I'm too old to be running after Stevie. I'm worn out after dealing with you when you were a teenager."

"Exactly! That's why I'm saying we're going to have to step in and fix things. I realize that you need my help with her. I'm gonna step up and help you 'cause something has to be done. I don't want her to go down the same path I did."

"You got that right."

"Mama, I'm about to go!" Stevie yelled from the living room.

"Oh, no you ain't!" Gwyn shouted.

"I'll be home in a few hours, ma!" Stevie ignored her sister and left out the door anyway.

"Did that heffa leave anyway?" Gwyn said appalled.

"Now you see what I have to deal with," Regina shook her head.

WHAT DID I DO TO
MAKE YOU HATE ME
SO MUCH?
-CHRIS BROWN, "I
CAN'T WIN"

CHAPTER 6

A million butterflies were fluttering around in Meesa's stomach as she prepared dinner. She couldn't stop her hands from shaking she was so nervous. She prayed that the camera men didn't pick up on her nervousness as she chopped up pieces of bacon to put into the chop salad she had prepared for dinner. On the menu that night was chop salad, warm, French bread and fried tilapia.

She knew that Black and the kids would enjoy it but she was unsure if Black's father would. He'd finally been released from prison. Black had gone to pick him up. Meesa was still unsure about having a murderer in her home. She didn't know this man from a can of paint and neither did her children. Their first encounter with their grandfather would either be a success or a complete disaster. Either way, it would all be caught on tape for her reality show.

Meesa tried to pretend that the cameras weren't there as she gazed around her beautiful, penthouse apartment. She and Black lived in the same building as Jay-Z and Beyoncé in Tribeca, New York. The building was very posh and elite. The building came equipped with a doorman, rooftop pool, gym, movie theater, bowling alley, restaurant and grocery store.

Meesa's apartment was immaculately decorated. It was chic as hell. The entire apartment had a modern/chic style to it. Meesa had a state-of-the-art kitchen. All of the appliances were stainless steel. In the center of the kitchen was an island with a glass bar top that added a sleek, smooth appeal to the space.

Black's father, Ron, would go from a tiny jail cell to living in a $10,000,000 swagged out apartment. It would be a complete culture shock. Meesa prayed that Black was making the right decision by letting his father live with them temporarily. Meesa didn't need any more drama in her life. She had enough on her plate already.

"Ma, I'm hungry. Can we eat yet or nah?" Kiyan groaned.

Meesa looked at her son. He was the spitting image of his father. Kiyan was a chocolate dream. He was 5'1 and possessed the smoothest cocoa skin she'd ever seen. He rocked a hi-top fade with three razor cut parts on the side. Like Black, he had almond-shaped eyes and full lips. Kiyan was growing up to be a handsome young man.

"How about I'ma beat yo' butt if you don't get out of them school clothes," she warned.

"Huuuuuuuh," Kiyan groaned, dragging his feet out of the room.

"Groan again and see what happen!" Meesa yelled over her shoulder.

"I keep tellin' y'all about that chile," Mila sauntered into the kitchen chewing a piece of gum like an around the way girl.

"Girl, hush," Meesa chuckled turning over a piece of fish.

Mila was a little spitfire. Meesa had gotten several offers from top modeling agencies for her to model but Meesa and Black wanted her to remain a child. Mila's mouth was already reckless enough. Meesa didn't know what to do with her. She was too smart for her own good. Mila's intelligence mixed with her quick wit and stunning looks was a lethal combination.

She had full, curly, natural hair that when flat ironed reached her butt. Her skin was the shade of black Hawaiian sand. Mila had her mother's hazel-green eyes. She also had a set of deep dimples and a smile that would brighten anyone's day. Meesa often caught herself in awe of the fact that she was her daughter. Kiyan and Mila were by far her two greatest creations.

"I'm just saying he stay hungry. I think he got a tapeworm." Mila sat at the kitchen island.

"Girl, ain't nothing wrong with that boy and what you know about a tapeworm?" Meesa took the pieces of fish out of the skillet and placed them on a paper towel.

"I learned about them in school, mommy."

"Ma, where pops at?" Kiyan returned to the kitchen.

"He went to go pick up our dinner guest," Meesa replied with a smile.

"Oooooh is it J. Lo? We had fun the last time she came over for dinner." Mila asked excitedly.

"Yeah, Jenny from the block butt was on swole for real." Kiyan looked at the ceiling and reminisced on her fatty.

"Boy, if you don't hush." Meesa furrowed her brows. "I swear if I didn't know any better, I would swear you two were raised by wolves."

"Ma, you have no chill." Kiyan shook his head as the front door opened.

Black walked in. Meesa's heart skipped a beat. After being together for over ten years, Black still made her melt inside whenever he was in her presence.

"Daddy!" Mila jumped down from the stool and ran over to him.

"Hey, daddy's baby." Black scooped her up in his arms.

"I missed you today, daddy." Mila hugged him around his neck.

"I missed you too, baby girl." Black kissed her on the cheek. "Meesa... Kiyan get in here! I got somebody I want y'all to meet!"

Meesa wiped her hand on a napkin and met Black in the living area.

"What up, pops?" Kiyan gave his father a pound.

Kiyan loved his father dearly. He was his idol. He emulated his every move. When he grew up he wanted to be just like his dad.

"What up, boy?" Black pulled his son close and hugged him.

"Hey, baby." Meesa gave Black a quick peck on the lips.

She was still tight about his announcement that he was getting back into the game, but for the sake of the kids, she put her feelings aside.

"Guys, I want you to meet somebody very special to me. Pop!" Black called out.

Black's father stepped inside with a small bag of items in his hand. Meesa couldn't believe her eyes. Ron, Black and Kiyan were identical. He was tall and dark as night. Ron had a lean, toned physique and a head full of grey hair that was cut low. Her heart instantly melted. It was refreshing to see three generations of Patterson men standing together.

"Hello, everyone." Ron spoke meekly.

He looked like a deer in headlights. His eyes grew wide as the camera crew invaded his personal space.

"Pops, is this your dad for real?" Kiyan quizzed stunned.

"Yes," Black responded.

"Dang, they finally let you out?" Mila exclaimed.

"Mila!" Meesa gasped.

"What? What I do?" Mila shrugged.

"This must be my granddaughter?" Ron chuckled.

"Pleasure to meet you, sir." Mila shook his hand and curtsied.

"Nice to meet you too, sweetheart." Ron kissed the outside of her tiny hand.

"Pop." Black pulled Meesa close. "This is my wife, Meesa."

"Hello," Meesa smiled brightly. "It's so good to finally meet you." Meesa gave him a warm hug.

She prayed that he couldn't see how nervous and uncomfortable she was. She was still very unsure of Ron living in their home.

"Let me take your things. Dinner is ready," Meesa smiled.

Ron handed his bag to her.

"You hungry as hell ain't you?" Mila said to her grandfather.

"Watch your mouth." Black lightly swatted her on the butt.

"Huuuuuh, why I always get in trouble for saying what everyone is thinking?" Mila rolled her eyes.

"This li'l girl gon' send me to an early grave," Black laughed.

"She's a beauty," Ron said endearingly.

"Grandpa, sit next to me," Kiyan requested pulling out his chair.

"Thank you."

"See… the kids are already taking to him. I told you that we had nothing to worry about." Black whispered into Meesa's ear.

"We'll see." Meesa went into the kitchen to grab the food.

Once everything was placed on the table, family style, Meesa took her seat. Black could tell that his dad was uncomfortable with the cameras being around.

"How was school today?" Black asked the kids as he placed his phones on the table.

Meesa looked at the phones out of the corner of her eye. She had no idea that Black had gone out and purchased two new cell phones.

"It was fine. Mr. Upchurch was up my ass— I mean up my butt." Kiyan corrected himself.

"Your kids sure do curse a lot," Ron chuckled.

"I don't know what's gotten into them today." Black mean mugged his kids.

"Before we eat let's all bow our heads." Meesa took Black and Mila's hand in hers.

Everyone else at the table held hands as well.

"Meesa, before you say grace can we get hair and makeup in here to touch you up?" Ian asked.

"Ummm," Meesa looked at Black. "Sure."

Black rolled his eyes and groaned. He was sick of these producers interrupting their lives for a good shot.

Once Meesa was touched up the producers instructed them to resume filming.

"Mila, you say grace tonight," Meesa said.

"I got you." Mila situated herself in her seat and cleared her throat.

"Blue Ivy, we come to you today."

"Mila," Meesa said firmly squeezing her hand.

"Huuuh… ok."

"Who is Blue Ivy?" Ron whispered to Black. "Is that some type of new religion?"

"No," Black laughed. "Blue Ivy is Beyoncé's daughter."

"Ohhhh," Ron nodded. "Who is Beyoncé?"

"Lord, forgive him because he knows not what he do," Mila shook her head.

"Mila, if you don't say grace," Meesa demanded.

"Lord, we thank you for watching over us today," Mila prayed sweetly. "We thank you for the blessing of us being able to sit here and have dinner once again as a family. We thank you for opening up the prison gates and allowing my dad's dad to come home. Lord Jesus, we thank you for my mommy's hands for they can sew a sickening outfit and cook a mean meal. Father God, we thank you for

my edges 'cause Lord, we know everybody ain't got'em—
"

"Wrap it up, Mila," Meesa said sternly.

"In Jesus' name we pray; amen." Mila opened her eyes with a huge smile on her face.

Meesa simply inhaled deeply and shook her head. Mila was a handful but she loved her dearly.

"Ok, guys, let's dig in." Meesa served dinner family style.

Everyone filled their plates with salad, fish and bread. Black's father especially filled his plate high. Meesa understood though. The man hadn't had a decent meal in years. Meesa watched closely as Ron took a bite of the fish. Ron closed his eyes and let the flavorful fish melt in his mouth.

"Is it good, Ron?" Meesa held her breath.

Ron opened his eyes, looked at Meesa and said, "Delicious."

"Good, I'm glad you're enjoying it," Meesa smiled, pleased with herself.

"I'm just glad you're finally home, pops." Black placed his arm around his father's shoulder and pulled him close.

"I know that things between us haven't always been good but now we can work on really rebuilding our relationship and getting you rehabilitated. I'm just happy that you're home. I know my mom is up in heaven smiling right now. She always wanted us to work things out," Black choked up.

Whenever he talked about his mother Black became emotional.

"You ok, baby?" Meesa rubbed his back.

"Yeah I'm good." Black swallowed the tears in his throat. "I'm just glad you're coming to live with us permanently, Pop. It's the best decision I have ever made."

"Permanently?" Meesa furrowed her brows confused.

They'd only discussed Black's father staying for a short period of time. Meesa had no plans for Ron's stay to be permanent.

"I'm sorry you guys." Ian chimed in again. "But, Black, can you say that speech again? It was riveting but Camera One didn't catch Meesa's reaction."

"Are you serious?" Black eyed Ian in disbelief.

His speech to his father was genuine and from the heart. It was something that couldn't be duplicated. Black wasn't the emotional type anyway, so for him to show emotion was a rarity.

"Yes we need that shot," Ian replied.

"What the fuck I look like to you, Denzel Washington? I ain't no actor," Black fumed.

"Baby, calm down," Meesa tried massaging the outside of Black's hand with her thumb to no avail.

"No, fuck that. I'm tired of this shit. Y'all gotta go." Black scooted his chair back and stood up.

"Baby, what are you doing?" Meesa stood up as well.

"I'm getting these muthafucka's outta my house!" He opened the front door.

"Stop cussing in front of the kids, Black!"

"This reality show shit is done, Meesa. I ain't feeling this shit no more. It's a wrap. Y'all get the fuck out!" He pushed the camera crew out one by one.

"Dad, stop!" Kiyan shouted.

"Black, you can't do that! I'm under contract. I'm so sorry you guys." Meesa apologized to the crew.

"Can we come back tomorrow?" Ian asked fumbling out the door.

Black lunged towards him and yanked Ian by his collar.

"Didn't I tell you filming was over?"

"Black, let him go now!" Meesa tried to pull him off Ian. "Ron, can you help me with your son?" She pleaded.

"Ah uh, I just got out of jail. I ain't going back." Ron added another piece of fish to his plate.

"Get off of me!" Ian yelled, trying to break loose.

"Dad, let him go!" Kiyan yelled rushing over to help his mother.

"Black, let go!" Meesa shrieked as Mila began to cry.

Hearing the sound of his baby girl crying brought Black to reality. He immediately let Ian go and regained his composure.

"If I see you on my door step it's gon' be a problem," Black warned the camera crew before slamming the door in their face.

"Mommy, daddy scared me!" Mila ran over to her mother and wept.

The kids had never seen their father act out so violently.

"It's ok, baby." Meesa held her daughter in her arms. "What the fuck is wrong with you? Why would you do that? They could sue me and you!" Meesa fumed.

"No they won't." Black paced back and forth.

"And how do you know this?"

Black stopped pacing and looked Meesa square in her eyes.

"Cause I'll make sure of it," he said coldly.

Meesa's heart immediately stopped beating. A cold sweat poured over her body. Black was insinuating that he would threaten to kill Ian. The kids didn't know what he meant 'cause they'd never seen their father in that light but the fact that he would even say something so vile in front of them was enough to send Meesa over the edge.

"In the bedroom now!" She snapped her finger and pointed. "Baby." She held Mila's face in the palm of her hands. "Mommy has to go talk to daddy. Go finish eating dinner, okay?"

"Yes. ma'am," Mila nodded her head.

Black followed Meesa down the hall to their room and closed the door behind him.

"Don't ever snap yo' fuckin' fingers at me like I'm a dog or a kid," he warned.

"Excuse you?" Meesa screwed up her face.

"You heard me." Black sat on the edge of the bed. "Now what is it? My food is getting cold."

Meesa stood back speechless. It was taking the will of God for her not to haul off and slap the shit outta him.

"What is your problem?" She finally asked.

"Every time I say something to you, you act like you're on your fuckin' period. If I breathe the wrong way, you get an attitude. If I try to talk to you, you get mad. Then you throw my film crew out. I mean, come on, Black. What is the deal?" Meesa spoke loudly forgetting that the kids and Ron could hear her.

"You already know what the deal is. I'm under a lot of stress." He glared at her.

"Mmm, what a surprise. Why don't you just back out now before it's too late? I'm sure he can ask somebody else to help him." Meesa spoke in code.

Setting aside her anger, she walked over and sat down on her knees before Black.

"We have a good life, babe," she stressed.

"You don't get it. You have a good life. We're living your dream. I don't want none of this shit and you know that. Me and you made a deal that once you established your career we would move our family back to St. Louis but look where we at… We still in New York and you know I hate it here. You couldn't even give me the one thing I wanted 'cause you're too busy trying to be the black Jessica Simpson."

"Wooow, so tell me how you really feel," Meesa scoffed.

"Are we done, 'cause I got my old dude in there waiting on me?" Black looked off to the side instead of giving Meesa eye contact.

"No, we're not done." She stood up.

"Speaking of your father, I never said that he could stay here permanently."

Black screwed up his face and looked up at Meesa.

"Man, you better get the fuck outta here wit' that shit. He's staying here. End of story."

"Black, please don't make me embarrass you 'cause I will go in there right now and tell him he has to go," Meesa challenged.

Black stood up and got in her face. In a low, menacing tone he replied, "Get fucked up if you want to. Don't ever fuckin' threaten me."

"It's not a threat. It's a promise." Meesa refused to back down.

She could tell that Black was at his limit with her but so was she with him.

"Oh ok," Black chuckled turning his back on her.

Meesa watched as he went into his private, walk-in closet. She had no idea what he was doing. Minutes later, Black walked back out with a leather MCM book bag. Black sat the bag on the bed and placed a few pair of underwear, his toothbrush and $50,000 in cash inside.

"What are you doing?" Meesa asked.

Black didn't even bother responding. Instead, he called for Kiyan to bring him his phone. Kiyan did as he was told and handed his father his cell phone.

"Can you and Ma please stop fighting so we can eat dinner like a family?" Kiyan pleaded.

"Just go back and eat your food, li'l man." Black kissed his son on the forehead.

Defeated, Kiyan walked back to the dining room. Black got on the internet and Googled Travelocity.

"What the fuck are you doing? Where are you going?" Meesa snapped.

Black still didn't respond.

"So you just gon' ignore me? You are so fuckin' childish." Meesa placed her hands on her hips.

Once Black's flight was booked, he grabbed his bag and bypassed Meesa. She followed angrily behind him.

"Black, I know you hear me talkin' to you?"

"Exactly, so why the fuck you keep talkin' to me," he barked. "Ay, daddy's about to go to St. Louis for a few days." Black grabbed one of his other phones from off the dining room table.

"Can we go?" Mila asked eagerly.

"No, daddy's going on business."

"Awww," Mila poked out her bottom lip.

"You two be good for mommy, ok?"

"Yes, sir," Kiyan replied sadly.

He hated when his parents fought which seemed to be all the time now.

"Pop, make yourself at home," Black patted his father on the back.

"Black, I know you're not about to leave," Meesa shot.

"I told yo' ass this ain't a game. You'll lose every time." Black unlocked the front door and left out.

"Oh word?" Meesa yelled after him. "Leave then! You better hope we're here when you get back!" She yelled as Black boarded the elevator.

Stunned that he actually just up and left, Meesa slammed the door shut and willed herself not to cry in front of the kids.

"This nigga got me fucked up." She ran over to the kitchen counter and grabbed her cell phone.

If Black thought that him leaving was the end of their conversation, then he had another thing coming. Meesa dialed his number ready to go off when she heard his phone vibrate on the dining room table. Black had taken his two new phones with him and left his old one at home on purpose. Meesa didn't have the numbers to the new phones so she had no way of contacting him. Pissed, Meesa took his phone and threw it against the wall, breaking it. Inhaling deeply, she turned to the kids and Black's father with a weird, Stepford Wife smile on her face and said, "Dessert anyone?"

I DON'T WANNA
HEAR A FUCKIN'
WORD WHEN YOU
SEE ME.
-CHRISS ZOE,
"HOMEBOY"

CHAPTER 7

Saturday nights, where Kelly could just chill at home with her son, pig out and watch television were nights she cherished. Normally her weekends were filled with dinner meetings, fancy parties or long nights at the office. That Saturday night she lay on the couch wrapped in a blanket, pigging out on spinach artichoke dip and Doritos. Her son sat on the floor in front of her playing with his Tonka trucks and WWE figurines.

Kelly loved spending time with her son. With her hectic schedule, she barely got to spend quiet moments with him. She tried to set aside mommy and son time at least once a week but something always ended up coming up. Her biggest fear was Jaden Jr. growing up and resenting her for working so much; but what was she to do?

Being the sole provider wasn't something she envisioned for herself but it was her reality. She didn't like it but what could she do? She couldn't break up with Jaden. Where would he go? He had no family in New York and very little back in St. Louis. Hell, he had no money, no job, no nothing. All he had was her and their son. She was tired of him going from job to job though.

Kelly prayed every night that he would come to his senses and get his shit together. She was over feeling like the man in their relationship. She wanted to feel taken care of and secure. It was fucked up to know that she had to provide her own security even though they'd been together for fifteen years. Kelly needed more and she was tired of begging for it. Crying, talking, praying and arguing - none of it seemed to work. She was at her wits end with Jaden.

"Ay yo, babe," Jaden came into the sitting room fully dressed to go out.

Although he worked her nerves, Kelly couldn't deny Jaden's sex appeal. He was 6'3 in height with a lean physique. His caramel complexion, full, coal black beard and sleeve full of tattoos gave him a bad boy edge. He stayed laced in the flyest gear. That night he donned a blue Think Smart snapback, white Bathing Ape tee-shirt, a pair of fitted jeans, Nike Foamposite sneakers and a simple, gold Rolex watch. However, Kelly found it funny that he could find the time to go out every weekend but couldn't find the time to get a job.

"What?" Kelly looked at him with a hint of annoyance in her eyes.

She already knew where this conversation was headed. Jaden was about to ask her for money so he could go out. He did it every weekend.

"What's wrong wit' you?" Jaden screwed up his face.

"Nothing, what is it?"

"Let me hold a few stacks."

Kelly inhaled deep and tried her hardest not to go off. This shit was old. Every weekend Jaden went to the club with a fresh, new haircut, fresh new fit, fresh new sneakers and a pocket full of cash which was all funded by Kelly. On the outside looking in, it seemed like he was doing the damn thing, but no, Jaden was a lazy-ass nigga that only wanted to stunt. He wasn't there financially or emotionally for his woman.

Kelly felt like she was going to lose her mind. This nigga got to do whatever he pleased. She never had a moment to herself to do anything. Life for her was always work and her son. Nobody ever thought about her wants and needs, especially not Jaden.

"How much money you need this week, Jaden?" She asked dryly.

"Why you say it like that?"

"'Cause I'm getting sick of lending yo' ass money all the time." Kelly snatched the blanket off of her and went to go grab her purse.

"Since when you lending me something? I thought we were in a relationship? I thought we were a family? You do for me. I do for you." Jaden followed her into the hallway.

"You don't do shit for me. When was the last time you took me out to dinner?" Kelly quizzed.

Jaden stood speechless.

"Exactly." Kelly rolled her eyes.

"Man, I swear it's a double standard with you. When I was holding down the fort while you went to school, which I paid for, you ain't have shit to say. When I was kicking you down stack after stack, taking you on shopping sprees, on vacation and moved us up here, I ain't never once come at you on sideways about no bread 'cause I loved you."

"And I love you too but that was nine years ago. I'm tired of hearing about a bunch of shit that happened in the early 2000's."

"Oh, so now it's terms and conditions on how long you supposed to hold ya' man down?"

"I don't have the time or the energy for this conversation." Kelly rummaged around her purse for some cash.

Instead, she found Dre's business card. She quickly dropped it back inside her purse so Jaden wouldn't see it.

"Here, just take the black card and please be mindful of how much you spend." She tossed the card at him.

"Yeah a'ight." Jaden sucked his teeth and left.

Kelly didn't even trip off the fact that he didn't say goodbye. She was just happy he was gone. She was determined not to let him ruin her night. Despite the constant sadness in her heart, she was determined to at least pretend like she was happy for the sake of her son. She never wanted him to see her sad and depressed. Mommy and son time was all about fun and laughter.

For the next few hours they did just that. They watched Frozen, sang along to all the songs and ate ice cream. After that, she bathed Jaden Jr., read him a bedtime story and put him to bed. Afterwards Kelly took a shower and curled up in bed. Before she knew it she was knocked out asleep. Kelly didn't even realize how tired she was until her head hit the pillow.

It was six o'clock the following morning when she woke up to go pee that she realized that Jaden still wasn't home. Kelly was disgusted. She was sick of babysitting a grown-ass man. This nigga couldn't even come home at a decent time. God knows what or who he was out doing. Kelly had no proof that he had ever cheated on her but she wouldn't be surprised if he had. Heated, she picked up the phone and called Jaden. The phone rang three times before she was sent to voicemail.

"Oh no the fuck he didn't," Kelly dialed his number again.

This time the phone barely rang once before she was hit with his voicemail. Jaden had turned his phone off.

"I am so over this shit," she snapped hanging up.

That was the last time she was going to allow Jaden to play her out. She was done playing the fool. Kelly was over feeling sorry for herself. It was time to take her life into her own hands and start doing her.

Gwyn lie butt naked under her Versace covers. Ferragamo lay next to her. She loved sleeping naked. She slept better naked. She wouldn't have it any other way. Her bare skin against the luxurious fabric comforted and soothed her. Plus she needed the rest. She'd been out the night before partying at Greenhouse with Nikki and OJ. They popped bottles with Rihanna, Drake and Cameron Diaz. They kicked it until the sun came up.

Afterwards, they all went and ate breakfast. She'd only gotten two hours of sleep when she heard loud, nonstop, animalistic moaning from the apartment above her. The shit had been going on for over a week. Apparently, the new tenants in the building loved to fuck. It seemed like whenever she was home they were having sex. Their freaky sexcapade's went on for hours too.

Gwyn tried to ignore the sounds by placing her pillow over her head but that didn't drown out the noise. They were so loud that Ferragamo had started to bark. If her ceiling wasn't so high and Gwyn knew where her maid kept the broom, she would bang on the ceiling. Gwyn looked at the clock. It was 9:10.

"Who is up fuckin' at this time of the morning," she groaned.

Gwyn was low-key kind of jealous that it wasn't her screaming to Jesus for more. Irritated and slightly turned on, she turned over onto her back and glared at the ceiling. She could hear the woman moaning, "Fuck me, fuck me!"

"Ferragamo, go to your bed," Gwyn ordered.

The dog did as he was told and hopped down from her bed and over to his.

Mad that she couldn't get any sleep and that it wasn't her getting her back cracked, Gwyn closed her eyes and allowed the erotic sounds to consume her. Before she knew it, her right hand had slipped under the covers and landed on the face of her pussy. Her fingers began to work magic on her clit. Gwyn imagined that it was her getting fucked. She imagined the man's long dick sliding in and out of her warm hole. She could almost feel him cupping her breasts and licking her neck. The more she imagined it, the more aroused she became.

"Ahhhhhhhh!" She heard the man growl.

Gwyn envisioned herself down on her knees taking the unknown man into her mouth. Her mouth began to water at the thought. The louder the couple moaned, the faster her fingers rotated. Gwyn rocked her hips back and forth and bit into her bottom lip. She was about to cum.

"Mmmmmmmmmm!" She whimpered as her juices spilled onto her fingertips.

Gwyn's eyes immediately popped open after she came. Panting, she gathered herself only to realize that the couple upstairs was still going strong. Irritated that they were still enjoying themselves and she wasn't, Gwyn hopped out of bed. Pissed, she slipped on a black, silk, spaghetti strap negligee and stormed out the door. She didn't care if the other tenants in the building saw her dressed scantily clad.

Gwyn loved her curvaceous frame. Taking the stairs, she raced to the 10th floor. Her titties bounced wildly as she raced to the noisy neighbor's door. Instead of ringing the door bell, Gwyn used her fist to knock. She wanted them to know she meant business. As she waited, she spotted the tenant down the hall by the name of Mrs. Finklestein come her way.

Mrs. Finklestein was the head of the apartment board. She was a filthy rich, stuffy, old broad. Every time she saw Gwyn she had something slick to say. As always, Mrs. Finklestein was dressed in head-to-toe Chanel. Gwyn was dying to get into her closet. Mrs. Finklestein had tons of dope, rare Chanel pieces but Mrs. Finklestein couldn't stand Gwyn. She found her to be classless, obnoxious, loud and crass.

"Good morning, Mrs. Finklestein." Gwyn pounded her fist once more against the door.

"Gwyneth, for God sake, stop all that pounding. I'm sure they can hear you all way in Brooklyn." Mrs. Finklestein grimaced.

"You don't hear them ravishing each other like two wild animals?" Gwyn spun around and faced Mrs. Finklestein.

"Can you and your dinosaur sized nipples please go back to your apartment?" Mrs. Finklestein eyed Gwyn up and down.

"I will as soon as I get them to be quiet."

"Mr. Warren is a fine young man. You leave him alone." Mrs. Finklestein swatted Gwyn on the butt with her purse. "And please go put some clothes on. You look like a porn star."

"Why thank you, Mrs. Finklestein. That's like the sweetest thing you've ever said to me," Gwen pretended to tear up as Mrs. Finklestein boarded the elevator.

Once the coast was clear, Gwyn resumed knocking on the door. Before she knew it, the door swung open and a gorgeous Brazilian woman stood before her dressed in only a towel. Her hair was wet and her entire body was dripping wet with water. Gwyn wasn't bi or gay but she would most certainly tap that ass. The chick was bad.

"Hola" The Brazilian hottie smiled brightly.

"Hi, I live in the apartment under you and I can hear you," Gwen replied.

"Eh," The Brazilian said not understanding Gwyn.

"I live under you." Gwyn spoke louder and pointed to the ground. "I can hear you having sex. Can you please quiet down some?"

"Uhhhh, me no understand." The Brazilian looked confused.

"I can hear you screwing!"

"Me no speak any English." The Brazilian shook her head.

"I can hear you fuckin'!" Gwyn made an O shape with her left hand and poked her right index finger through it repeatedly.

"Ohhhhhhhhh." The Brazilian laughed. "You join?" She dropped her towel revealing a stunningly flawless body.

"Oh my God." Gwyn covered her eyes with her hand. "Please put your towel back on."

"Baby, who is that at the door?" Gwyn heard a familiar voice say.

Perplexed, she uncovered her eyes and watched as the man of the house came from around the corner. Low and behold, she made eye contact with Cash.

"You're Mr. Warren?" She shrieked stunned.

"Yeah." He answered shocked to see her as well. "What are you doing here?" He tightened the towel around his waist.

"I live on the 9th floor, stalker!"

"I'm far from a stalker, sweetheart," Cash grinned.

"Yeah right; like you didn't know I stayed in this building." Gwyn eyed him with disgust and lust at the same time.

Cash's body was rippled with muscles. He looked like a black and Asian superhero. He had a lean physique but his stomach held a perfect eight pack. Gwyn didn't know if she wanted to lick him, hit him, bite him or fuck him. Knowing that Cash was banging another chick's back out annoyed the hell out of her. The way he'd been sweating her she thought he was all about her but obviously not.

"I had no idea you stayed here," Cash said truthfully. "Bebé puesto en tu toalla." Cash told the Brazilian to put back on her towel.

"What the fuck you just say?" Gwyn snapped assuming he was talking about her. "You know what, that don't even matter. Whether you knew is neither here nor there. For the past week I have been hearing you two fucking like wild animals and frankly, I'm sick of it."

"What you want me to say; my bad?" Cash asked with a laugh.

"I want you to shut the hell up so I can get some sleep. Ok?" Gwyn smirked before turning her back on him and walking away.

Later that day, after getting a few hours of peaceful sleep, Gwyn got dressed so she could head out to grab a bite to eat and do a little light shopping. She was casually dressed in a white camisole, no bra, skin tight, white, skinny leg jeans and flip flops. Her long, black hair was pulled up into a messy bun. Gwyn wore her favorite white, Chanel quilted, cross body purse as she headed to board the elevator. Little did she know, as soon as she hopped onto the elevator she would run into Cash for the second time that day?

"Oh God not you again," she groaned, pressing the garage button.

"You know you're happy to see me." Cash leaned against the elevator frame and eyed her lustfully.

Gwyn's body was ridiculous. She was tall with perky, large breasts, curvaceous hips and a round ass. Cash wanted nothing more than to stop the elevator and take her right then and there. He controlled his urges and continued to play it cool though. He would never admit it to Gwyn because of his pride but he felt some type of way about her not answering or returning any of his calls. It was obvious that they had chemistry.

Why she was being so difficult he would never understand. From the moment he laid eyes on her again she hadn't left his mind. He thought about her day and night. Since she wouldn't give him the time of day, Cash preoccupied his time with Esperanza. Whenever they had sex he imagined that he was making love to Gwyn but there was nothing like having the real thing.

"Where you headed?" He quizzed as she pushed the button for the elevator door to close.

"To my car," Gwyn replied like he was stupid.

"That's funny; I am too."

Gwyn quickly glanced over at Cash and rolled her eyes at him. How dare he look that damn cute on a Sunday afternoon? Cash seemed to get hotter and hotter every time she saw him. The physical attraction she had for him was unparallel to any other man she'd ever encountered.

"Listen, my bad for all the noise. I had no idea that anyone could hear us," Cash apologized.

"It's cool," Gwyn replied, feeling herself tense up.

The mere mention of him having sex with another woman gave her anxiety.

"I mean, in the future, what would you like for me to do?" Cash asked, fucking with her. "Should I move my bed, turn on some music, put a muzzle on the chick? What would make you feel more comfortable?"

"How about you stop fucking other chicks period," Gwyn snapped as the elevator doors opened.

Switching her hips, she glided over to her car.

"Don't tell me you're jealous?" Cash questioned unknowingly parked next to her. "You want me to fuck you?"

This nigga got nerve, Gwyn thought sucking her teeth.

"Honey, if I wanted to fuck you, I would've answered your calls." She shot getting inside her car.

Flabbergasted by her response, Cash stood speechless. He wanted to hit her with a snappy comeback but what was there say? Gwyn had him in the palm of her hand and didn't even know it. Cash wasn't sure what he had to do but Gwyn was gonna be his.

I THOUGHT I'D NEVER
SEE THIS PLACE AGAIN.
I THOUGHT I'D NEVER
SEE THIS SPACE AGAIN,
YET HERE I AM.
-ALEX ISLEY, "SO HERE
IT GOES"

CHAPTER 8

Meesa sat with her knees up to her chest gazing blankly at the floor. Once again she'd greeted the sun. Rays from the morning sun shown brightly. She sat on her side of the bed wishing Black was on his but he wasn't. He was gone. The fear that she was losing her husband consumed every crevice of her being. She hadn't spoken to him once since he'd left. He'd been gone two days now. She hadn't slept a wink since. Sleep was the last thing on her mind, it had become her enemy.

The past two days had been the longest two days of her life. Meesa hated going to work. For eight hours she had to pretend like her life wasn't hanging on by a thread. No one knew that her life was falling apart. She wanted to tell her friends but Meesa had learned from past experiences to keep her relationship problems to herself. Her friends had a way of only hanging on to the negative things and not the positive things about her relationship.

She and Black had gone through worse. They'd get through this rough patch. At least that's what she told herself.

Things had never gotten so bad that he just up and left. Meesa didn't know what that was about. She knew he had business in St. Louis but their marriage was far more important than some stupid-ass drug transactions. It was obvious by his disrespectful behavior that Black felt differently about her. Meesa placed her head in her lap. Her head wouldn't stop spinning. All she kept thinking was that when it rained it poured.

Since Black left, she'd been going through it. She wanted her husband back home where he belonged. Meesa didn't want to reveal that there was trouble in paradise but she had to find out Black's whereabouts. She picked up the phone and called her sister. She hoped Mina was up. It was 6:30am in St. Louis.

"Hello?" Mina answered the phone on the second ring.

"Hey, did I wake you?"

"No, I was already up getting the kids ready for school. What's up?"

"Nothing, I was just calling to see if you had spoken to Black?"

Meesa felt so stupid asking the question. It was obvious that she didn't know where her husband was.

"Yeah. He came by here yesterday to check on a few things." Mina spoke in code.

"Ok, I was just wondering." Meesa's heart started beating at a normal pace.

"Is everything alright? You don't sound too good," Mina asked concerned.

"Yeah, I'm fine. We just had a little argument, that's all. He call his self being mad at me but he'll be alright," Meesa played it off.

"Oh, 'cause he seemed fine when I saw him."

"That's good to know," Meesa said sarcastically.

It pissed her off that Black was off acting like their beef wasn't tearing him up inside. Hell, maybe it wasn't. Maybe Meesa was the only one distraught over their argument.

"I'm sorry to be calling you with my drama," she apologized. "You over there dealing with so much and I'm over here tripping off my mess. How are you?"

"Uhhhhhh… I'm surviving. I just want my husband to come home. I miss him terribly," Mina confessed.

"I know the feeling," Meesa agreed. "Well, I'm not going to keep you. Kiss my niece and nephew for me. I gotta get off my butt up and get my own damn kids off to school."

"Tell Kiyan and Mila I love them and call me if you need to talk, ok?"

"I will. I love you, sis," Meesa said.

"I love you too." Mina ended the call.

Meesa let out a sigh of relief. At least she knew Black was ok and was where he said he would be. Now it was just a waiting game as to when he'd be returning home. Meesa eased out of bed and placed on her slippers. She was already dressed in a cashmere, oversized tank top and leggings. Before she left her bedroom she examined her face in the mirror.

She couldn't let the kids see the distress she felt on her face. She had to make them feel like everything was ok. Maybe if she convinced them she'd be able to convince herself. Meesa walked down the hall and her nose was instantly engulfed with the smell of bacon frying. She was confused as to who would be up cooking breakfast. To her surprise, when she entered the kitchen she found Ron at the stove whipping up bacon, scrambled eggs, grits and toast. The kids were at the kitchen island dressed in their school uniform, finishing up their homework from the night before.

"Morning, mommy," Mila spoke cheerfully.

"Hi, baby." Meesa walked over and placed a loving kiss on her forehead. "Morning, son." She hugged Kiyan tight.

"Oww, ma, you gon' mess up my box," Kiyan frowned.

"Aww, hush! Yo' li'l funky hair will be a'ight." Meesa playfully pushed him.

"Good morning, Ron." Meesa stood next to him and gave him a one arm hug. "I didn't know you were cooking breakfast. I would've helped you."

"It's fine. I hope you didn't mind me taking it upon myself to cook. I just figured you may need the help with all that's going on." Ron gave her a warm smile.

"Thank you. That's very sweet of you," Meesa replied, genuinely touched. "I was in no mood to cook this morning."

"I figured. Have you talked to my son?" Ron asked in a low tone so that the kids couldn't hear.

"No, he hasn't called me once," Meesa whispered back.

"He called me," Mila announced, eavesdropping.

"When?" Meesa whipped around shocked.

She naturally assumed that if Black hadn't called her that he hadn't called the kids either.

"This morning."

"He called me too," Kiyan declared.

"I talked to him last night," Ron confessed feeling bad for Meesa.

"So he's called everybody but me?" Meesa said out loud to herself.

"Apparently," Mila chuckled with mock sarcasm.

"Hand me your phone." Meesa held out her hand.

She wanted to see what number Black called the kids from. Mila handed her mom her phone. Meesa went through Mila's call log and saw that Black called from a private number. He was doing everything in his power for Meesa to be unable to contact him.

"What did he say when he called?" She asked, handing Mila back her phone.

"He said that he missed us and that he was going to bring us some stuff back when he comes home."

"When will that be?" Meesa asked curiously.

"He didn't say all of that. Mommy, you really need to get your life in order," Mila said sounding like a mini Tamar Braxton. "Get control of your husband. He got you out here lookin' crazy, girl."

Meesa wanted to check her daughter for being too grown but in all actuality, Mila had a point. Meesa looked like an absolute fool asking her kids where their father was. She couldn't believe that Black had put her in such a fucked up position. If he wanted to act like a fool then so be it. Meesa couldn't continue to concentrate on Black and his idiotic behavior. She had a fashion show to worry about it.

I COULD HIT YO' TYPE
WITHOUT THE HAT.
-SCHOOLBOY Q,
"STUDIO"

CHAPTER 9

It was a typical weekday. Kelly was in Jaden Jr.'s room picking out an outfit for him to wear to preschool. Picking out an outfit for him to wear was the highlight of her morning. She loved dressing him up in cute, little outfits. Jaden Jr. was the flyest little boy in preschool and the smartest. Kelly prided herself on giving him the best education money could buy. She already had him taking piano and Spanish lessons.

"You want me to take him to school?" Jaden came and stood in the doorway.

Kelly pretended that he wasn't even there. She didn't have shit to say to him. Ever since Jaden didn't come home that Saturday night, Kelly had been giving him the silent treatment. If he had the balls to stay out all night and not answer her calls, then he didn't deserve to be acknowledged by her. Kelly was over the games and shenanigans. She was sick of Jaden's childish, immature behavior. Jaden not coming home was the last straw. She'd had enough.

"Come here, baby." Kelly got down on her knees and helped Jaden Jr. into his clothes.

That day he would be rocking Givenchy.

"I can help you get him dressed," Jaden continued.

"Mama, I'm hungry. I want some cereal," Jaden Jr. yawned.

"I'll fix him a bowl." Jaden declared heading to the kitchen.

He had to make things right with Kelly. He hadn't meant to stay out that night and come in the next day. After the club let out, he and his pot'nahs hit up the strip club then a local diner for breakfast. Jaden was having so much fun that he'd lost track of time. When Kelly called him he sent her to voicemail because he didn't feel like arguing. He knew she was going to have an attitude. He was high and kicking it. He wasn't about to let Kelly blow his high.

Now he was paying for it. Kelly wasn't speaking to him and he no longer had access to any of her accounts. He was a man dangling from a cracked limb. Jaden needed Kelly more than she needed him and she knew it. Because of his nonexistent financial status he couldn't survive without her so he couldn't lose her.

And yeah, he still cared for her but the love between he and Kelly had begun to fade years ago. They were basically coexisting for the sake of their son. Jaden needed a roof over his head and food to eat, so he was going to kiss as much ass as necessary in order to get back into her good graces.

Kelly finished getting Jaden Jr. dressed then sent him into the kitchen to eat breakfast. Back in her bedroom she sat at her vanity and applied her makeup. Kelly was halfway finished when she received an inbox from Facebook. She opened the app and found that she had a message from Dre. *This man just won't quit,* she thought reading the message.

<Back   **Dre**

Active now

Morning, beautiful, you done playin' house yet?

Sent from mobile

Kelly couldn't help but smile. *Maybe* she replied.

<Back   **Dre**

Active now

Oh word?

Yeah. Shouldn't u be working? Why r u up at
this time of morning inboxing me?

I'm actually out of the country. It's nighttime
here. I couldn't stop thinkin' about u...

Kelly grinned from ear-to-ear. She had no idea that
Jaden had reentered the room and was watching her every
move. *What the fuck is she smiling about,* he thought. *Just
a minute ago she was walking around mad at the world.*

"Kelly." He tried to get her attention.

But Kelly was so enthralled in her conversation that
she didn't even hear him calling her name. At least she
pretended not to.

<Back   **Dre**

Active now

Aww that's sweet... game but sweet

I don't run game, sweetheart... When I get

back in town let's link up

Kelly inhaled deep before responding. If she met up with Dre she was sure to give into temptation. He was way too fine not to. Plus, to have the pleasure of a man's welcomed attention was ego boosting. It felt great to be wanted by a man.

<Back   Dre   ②
Active now

Ok

"Kelly! I know you hear me!" Jaden barked.

"What?!" Kelly snapped back to reality. "What do you want?"

"Who you over there talkin' to?" Jaden fumed.

"None of yo' damn business." Kelly screwed up her face.

"Whoever it is got you over there smiling and shit. Let me find out you fuckin' wit' somebody else." Jaden warned.

"And what you gon' do?" Kelly rolled her neck. "Not a goddamn thing. Shit…Why are you even talking to me?" She threw down her blush brush.

"I don't fuck wit' you! What about that don't you get? Leave me alone!" She shot storming into the bathroom and slamming the door behind her.

"I been drankin'… I been drankin'." Gwyn held up her fifth shot of Patron.

It was Friday and Friday's for Gwyn meant turn up time. The stress of the workweek was over. She could let her hair down and vibe out with her girls, which was always fun. Gwyn, Nikki and Destiny sat throwing back shots at one of New York's premiere bars. Earl's Beer & Cheese was tucked between the Upper East Side and Spanish Harlem. It was a craft beer cubbyhole with well-priced beer. The highlight of the bar was the NY State Cheddar grilled cheese sandwich with braised pork belly, a fried egg and homemade kimchi.

Earl's Beer & Cheese was one of Gwyn's favorite places to go and chill. Gwyn loved to kick it. The older she got, the harder it was to pull her girls out of the house on the weekends. They were always boo'd up with their men. Gwyn barely had anyone to kick it with anymore. Now that

Nikki was officially off the market, Gwyn found herself the only single girl out the click.

Gwyn cherished her singledom. She could come and go as she pleased. She didn't have to worry about anyone nagging her about her whereabouts or who she was with. She could do what she wanted. Her rolodex of men to call when she wanted some male attention stayed full. Gwyn had a different man for every day of the week. But on nights like this where she was rocking one of the shortest skirts in her closet and heels that glittered underneath the moonlight, all she wanted was to kick it with her girls.

Nikki and Destiny had other plans though. It was going on 1:00am and they were ready to turn in. They tried to pretend like they were tired but Gwyn knew better. She knew their asses weren't tired. They were just trying to get home to the dick that was awaiting them. Gwyn wanted to hate but she couldn't. If she had something hot waiting for her she'd leave too.

"Ok, I'm about to get out of here." Nikki announced grabbing her Fendi clutch purse.

"C'mon, at least have one more drink with me," Gwyn begged.

"Nigga, no. I'm already drunk as it is."

"Huuuuuh… suck balls. You are so not fun," Gwyn remarked. "Destiny, I know you'll have another drink with me."

"Uh no, I won't. My boo-kitten is waiting outside in the car." She referred to Kat.

"I hate you two in-love bitches. I'ma find me some new friends."

"Good luck with that." Nikki hugged Gwyn goodbye from behind. "We barely tolerate yo' ass."

"Ha ha, funny." Gwyn flicked her off.

"Bye, girl," Destiny waved goodbye.

"Bye, heffa," Gwyn sulked.

She watched with envy as the girls left to go be with their men. In no mood to turn in, Gwyn signaled the bartender.

"Yes," he smiled.

"Let me get a vodka and cranberry."

"Coming right up."

As Gwyn awaited her next drink, she pulled out her iPhone and scrolled through her contact list. She was going to find somebody to kick it with if it was the last thing she did. Only one person came to mind. She knew she had no business hitting him up due to their circumstances but she only wanted to be with him.

<Messages   **Never Call**   Contact

Come have a drink wit' me

A few minutes later Cash responded.

<Messages   **Never Call**   Contact

Come have a drink wit' me

Where?

Gwyn gave him the name and location. A short while later, Cash entered Earl's looking like a bag of money. His entire presence filled the room. Cash's style game was on ten that night. He wore a black bowler hat, black Supreme tee-shirt, black jeans and black Tim's. Around his neck was a gold chain. His tattoos and overall sex appeal made Gwyn's pussy cream. She started to wonder if inviting him out was a smart thing to do. Upon sight, all she could think about was him bending her over the bar and fucking the shit outta her.

"What's up, beautiful?" He sat down next to her. "You started drinking without me?"

"I been drankin'... I been drankin'," Gwyn sang. "You better catch up."

"Oh you toasted." Cash laughed noticing how tipsy she was.

"I'm grooving."

"Can I get you something to drink, sir?" The bartender asked Cash.

"I'll have what she's having." Cash looked over at Gwyn and admired how beautiful she was.

Gwyn was an effortless beauty. She didn't have to do much to stand out in the crowd. The light inside of her shined from the inside out. Cash watched intently as she tossed her hair over her shoulder. Her follicles of hair brushed against her skin as she looked into his eyes and smiled brightly. She didn't have to say it. He knew that she was happy to see him. He could tell by the flicker of joy in her eyes.

"Here you go." The bartender handed him his drink. "Aren't you Cash?"

"Yeah," Cash grinned.

He never got used to people noticing him.

"Aww shit, damn. I love your music, man."

"Thanks, bro."

"Can I have your autograph?"

"I got you." Cash scribbled his name on a napkin and handed it to him. "Now back to you, beautiful."

"Let's make a toast." Gwyn faced him.

"A toast to what?" Cash held up his glass mesmerized by her every move.

Gwyn thought for a minute.

"Let's toast to freedom," she beamed.

"To freedom." Cash clicked his glass against hers then took a drink. "You're a wild one, huh?"

"You can't tell?" Gwyn took a sip of her drink.

"I can tell; that's what scares me."

"Why does it scare you? 'Cause you can't control me? 'Cause I don't fawn over you and hang onto your every world like the Brazilian? Speaking of the Brazilian, where is she?" Gwyn looked around in search of her.

"I don't know, you tell me," Cash countered. "For your information, I don't want to control you. I honestly just wanna understand you."

"You'll never understand me. Hell, I don't even understand me most of the time. I'm very complicated."

"Tell me about it. The last time I saw you, you were cussing me out."

"Quit over exaggerating," Gwyn giggled. "I didn't cuss you out. I gave you a piece of my mind."

"What made you hit me up tonight? When I was hitting you up you act like you ain't wanna be bothered."

"It's not that I didn't wanna be bothered. I just have a lot going on right now."

"We all have a lot going on," Cash challenged.

"Yeah, but my life right now is very full."

"Talk to me. What's going on?" Cash tried to get to know her on a deeper level.

He wanted to know everything about her. He wanted to make up for all the time they'd spent apart. He had his dream girl back and he didn't want to lose her. He wanted to drown in her every word and wade in her laughter if she'd let him.

Gwyn gazed at Cash. She could tell by the eagerness in his eyes that he hung off her every word. Normally she would view this as a sign of weakness and use it to her advantage. But Gwyn couldn't play Cash. Keeping her distance was the best thing but thoughts of him constantly invaded her mind. She wanted to open up to him but doing so would bring major complications. She had to keep him at arm's length.

"I don't wanna talk about me tonight." Gwyn placed her hands on Cash's thighs. "As a matter-of-fact, I don't wanna talk at all. I only have one question."

"What's that?" Cash asked as Gwyn leaned over and got into his face.

Her lips were inches away from his.

"You wanna fuck or nah?" Gwyn licked his bottom lip with her tongue.

Cash and Gwyn didn't even finish their drink after that. Before either of them knew it, they were at her crib ripping each other's clothes off. Gwyn kicked the door open as Cash tore off her top. She wore no bra so her breasts spilled out into the atmosphere. Cash quickly unbuttoned his jeans and placed her up against the wall.

Gwyn hungrily kissed his lips. Cash released his lips from her and palmed her throat as he inserted himself deep inside her sugar walls. The first stroke felt like heaven and hell wrapped up in one.

"Ahhhhhhhhhhhh! Yes," Gwyn moaned. "Fuck me."

Cash gripped her thighs and pumped in and out of her at a feverish pace. Gwyn's pussy was spellbinding. He could become lost in it if he stayed in it too long. But the thing was, he already wanted to stay in it forever. With one stroke he'd become addicted.

"Damn this shit feels good," he groaned.

"You like that, baby?" Gwyn panted. "You like that wet pussy, don't you?" She swirled her tongue across her lip as he watched on in agony.

"Yes." Cash pumped harder.

"You wanna cum, don't you?" She whimpered.

"No," Cash rotated his hips in a circular motion. "I'ma stay up in this shit all night."

"You promise?" Gwyn's lips trembled.

Her body was becoming weak. She could hardly breathe. Cash's dick was hitting her spine. She could feel it.

"You gon' stop runnin'?" Cash asked feeling his self about to cum.

Gwyn wanted to say no, but after receiving the dick down of her life, there was no way she could lie. Cash was that deal. He was fine, could fuck and had dough. Cash was the holy grail of niggas. He was a rarity. She had to hold onto to him if for nothing else but the dick.

"Yes!" Gwyn screamed, cumming all over his dick.

ACT LIKE AN ADULT.
HAVE AN AFFAIR FOR
ONCE.
-MYA FEAT. JAY-Z, "BEST
OF ME-PART 2"

CHAPTER 10

Black inhaled the end of summer St. Louis air. He took the city in one breath at a time. He loved being home. St. Louis was the only home he knew. In New York he felt like a visitor. Although New York was considered one of the world's premiere destinations, Black would choose St. Louis over it anytime. He knew the streets like he knew the back of his own hand.

All of his homeboys from the old neighborhood, except Kat, were there. He missed the comradery, the down home feel and food. St. Louis had the best Chinese food in the United States. That day Black stood in the parking lot in North Oaks Plaza, leaning against his rental car eating a box of special fried rice. He knew that he should've checked in with Meesa by now but Black needed time to clear his mind. He didn't feel like arguing with her again. He'd deal with Meesa when he returned home.

Black and his homeboy Dutch were shooting the breeze when a white Range Rover pulled up blasting the new Jeezy album. Black cut his eyes at the driver as she hopped out. The chick was bad and the epitome of ghetto fabulousness. She was 5'5 with caramel colored skin. She rocked a black, 33 inch, U-Part wig. On her full lips was M.A.C's Candy Yum Yum lipstick. The chick didn't care that it was a regular Tuesday afternoon. She showcased her toned physique by rocking a neon green bralette and matching joggers. On her feet were a pair of nude, Manolo Blahnik ankle strapped heels.

"What up, fellas?" The woman spoke giving Black a kiss on the cheek.

"What's good?" Black gave the woman a one arm hug.

"You got that for me, daddy?"

Black reached inside his back pocket and pulled out a wad of money. The woman happily took the stack of dough from his hand.

"Thank you, baby." She winked her eye before heading back to her ride.

Black continued on with his conversation and thought about the turn up that was going to ensue later on that week.

Kelly's heart beat a mile a minute. She hadn't been this nervous since high school when she met Jaden. Butterflies filled the pit of her stomach as she waited with baited breath for Dre to arrive. They'd made plans to meet up for coffee in Central Park. The day couldn't have been better. It was beautiful outside. The sun was out and it was a cool 62 degrees.

Kelly sat on a park bench with two cups of Starbucks coffee in her hand. She'd gotten them both decaf. She hoped that was how he took his coffee. Kelly situated herself on the bench. She'd been practicing her pose for the past ten minutes. She wanted to look perfect when Dre arrived. She wanted to seem cool and unaffected. She didn't want to come across eager or anxious.

Kelly knew that she didn't have any business being there. Sure, she no longer loved Jaden but they hadn't officially broken things off. Plus, they had a child together. Jaden was all she knew. He was the only man she'd ever been with but she was sick of dealing with his bullshit. She was way too successful to be settling for less. Kelly just had to get the courage to say enough was enough and leave.

Looking to her left she spotted Dre coming her way. Kelly's mouth instantly began to salivate. She damn near dropped the coffee on her lap she was so mesmerized by his sex appeal. Dre looked sexy as hell in a Brunello Cucinelli two-button check suit jacket, white shirt, brown tie and five-pocket, cotton-wool pants. She prayed to God that he thought she looked equally as nice. Kelly wasn't flashy or overtly sexual with her style.

She never dressed to be sexy. She was always very modest. It had taken her hours just to pick out her look that morning. She'd finally settled on a leather moto jacket, burgundy and white Stella McCartney blocked shift dress and Valentino rockstud calf hair ankle-strap pumps. A simple pair of black, wafer shades and a gold Cartier watch completed her look.

"Hi." She rose to her feet.

"Sorry I'm late." Dre greeted her with a warm hug.

"It's ok. You're just a few minutes late. Don't make it a habit though," she half joked.

"Damn, you went from giving me your ass to kiss to now making plans to see me again," he grinned.

"Don't flatter yourself. We can easily go back to me giving you my ass to kiss." Kelly shot defensively.

Dre looked at her like she was crazy.

"My bad. I ain't mean to offend you." He released her from his grasp. "I was just joking around."

Kelly gathered her composure.

"I'm sorry." She sat back down.

"I'm just a little bit on edge. I've never done this before," she confessed.

"Done what?" Dre sat down next to her.

"Here," Kelly handed him his cup of coffee.

"Thank you."

"I've never had an affair before." Kelly whispered as if anyone could hear her.

Dre burst out laughing.

"What's so funny?" Kelly asked with an attitude.

"I didn't know we were having an affair. I thought we were just having coffee," he chuckled.

Kelly's face turned beet red. She felt like a complete idiot. She thought Dre was into her. Had she read him wrong?

"So wait a minute. Let me get this straight. You ain't checkin' for me? You don't like me?"

"I barely even know you."

"Then what the hell am I doing here?" Kelly exclaimed perplexed. "This is stupid and a waste of my time. I gotta go." She tried to get up but Dre eased her back down.

"Stop it. You gon' give yourself an aneurism. Stop overreacting all the time. All I'm saying is I'm trying to get to know you. If I didn't like you, I wouldn't be here. You're a beautiful woman, Kelly, so of course I'm trying to get next to you." Dre leaned over and kissed her softly on the lips.

Kelly's whole entire body trembled at his touch. Dre's tongue tasted like wine. She wanted to drown in his nectar.

"Dre, stop." She leaned back coming to her senses.

She was out in broad daylight kissing another man.

"I can't do this."

Dre ignored her protest and continued to assault her lips with passionate kisses.

"Come here." He lifted her up on her feet.

Dre led her over to a secluded area of the park, right under the bridge. He placed Kelly's back up against the cobblestone. She didn't know what was happening but was enjoying every minute. Dre slipped his hand underneath her dress and ripped off her panties.

"Ahhhhhh!" Kelly gasped.

She was afraid and turned on at the same time

"What are you doing?" She asked short of breath. "Somebody might see."

"That's the point." Dre grabbed her by the throat and placed his lips upon hers.

Kelly instantly thought about screaming for help until he placed a trail of kisses from her lips down to the inner part of her thighs. Kelly was spellbound. She'd never had sex outdoors before. She never even expected when she met up with him that this would be the outcome of their date. She figured it would be a minute before they got physical. But here she was in the middle of the park with his face in-between her thighs.

Kelly looked down at the top of his and moaned. Dre's head was moving around in a circular motion. Her right leg was draped over his shoulder. Dre's tongue was working magic on her pussy. If his tongue went any further inside her slit he was sure to drown. Kelly was at the brink of no return. Jolts of electricity shot throughout her stomach causing her stomach to contract.

"Ahhhhhhhhhhhhhhhhhhhhhhhhh!" She clenched her eyes shut.

Dre's tongue was flickering across her clit at lightening speed. Kelly rubbed the top of his head. She opened her eyes and found a woman jogger staring at her. This turned Kelly on even more. She never knew she'd get off on people watching her having sex but she loved it. Before she knew it, she'd cum inside Dre's mouth and slapped high-fives with Jesus. Dre's wicked tongue had entrapped her. Kelly wanted more.

ME BEING WHEREVER
I'M AT, WORRIED
ABOUT WHEREVER
YOU ARE.
-BEYONCÉ FEAT.
DRAKE, "MINE"

CHAPTER 11

With everything that Meesa had going in her life, New York Fashion Week trumped everything. It was the day of her showing. Backstage was pure chaos. Models, makeup artist, hairstylist, seamstress and staff were running around like chickens with their heads cut off. Normally, Black would be there to ease her fears but this year Meesa had to go at it alone.

She knew that her friends noticed that he was absent but like true friends, they said nothing. For Meesa's sake, no one said a word. She was already under enough stress. She didn't need any added drama to her plate. Thankfully, her family wasn't there to witness the demise of her marriage. With Victor M.I.A., Mina decided to stay at home. Meesa's father had the flu so he couldn't come either.

Meesa stood off to the side. She'd shown at Mercedes Benz Fashion Week numerous times but each time was always like her first. She was always worried that her collection would flop and that the critics would hate it.

Meesa wouldn't be able to handle it if that happened. Black giving her the silent treatment was enough torture for her.

"Girl, it is a packed house," Gwyn exclaimed.

"Are all the seats filled?" Meesa said at once.

"Yes."

"Is Anna here yet?" Meesa referred to Vogue editor-in-chief, Anna Wintour.

"Yes, girl, and serving resting bitch face for the gawds," Gwyn snapped her fingers.

"Where is Kelly?"

"Greeting all of the buyers."

"Good. Are all of the models ready?"

"Yes, girl, calm down," Gwyn said with a slight laugh.

"Okay, well let's get them lined up so we can start the show." Meesa held Gwyn's hands and jumped up and down with glee.

Gwyn rounded up all of the models and had them line up in order. Meesa went down the line and did last minute touches to each girl's look. Her 2015 spring/summer collection was filled with curve-skimming dresses and underwear-inspired pieces. Meesa's inspiration was the Spanish invasion of Sicily, which began in the 15th century.

Models wore black, matador-style jackets, fringed capes, flamenco-style, layered, polka dot dresses and white bullfighter shirts tucked into satin, embellished bloomers. Shoes were embellished with rivets and gold hearts to ornate a sumptuous effect. All of the girls looked beautiful, especially Destiny. She would be the last model to hit the runway. She was wearing Meesa's finale piece which was a dramatic red gown with a ruffled, layered bottom.

It was her wow piece. She'd been working on it for months. It was the star of the entire collection and Black wouldn't even be there to see the finished product. He wouldn't even be there to see her and the kids walk down the runway at the end of the show. It was their family tradition. She'd walk down the runway hand-in-hand with the kids, halfway down, Black would stand up and present her with a bouquet of her favorite flowers.

This year, however, would be different. Meesa was sure the press would notice Black's absence. By the next morning whispers of marriage troubles would be all over the press. Meesa would have to do damage control and quick. As the music cued and the first model stepped onto the runway, Meesa signaled for Nikki to come over. Nikki was Meesa's and the company's publicist.

"You look gorgeous, pretty girl," Nikki admired Meesa's outfit.

Meesa looked absolutely stunning in a red Miss A halter neck, burnout velvet and chiffon, open back gown. The gown hugged all of her curves in the right spots. The A-line skirt fell to floor. A mini train cascaded behind her. Her short, platinum blonde hair was slicked down with a deep side part. She wore minimal makeup. Lime Crime's Salem lip stain set her entire look off.

"Thank you. You look great as well. Look, as soon as the show is over, I'm going to need for you to get on the phone and give an explanation as to why Black's not here," Meesa whispered.

"Why isn't he here? He never misses a show." Nikki died to know.

"He's away on business but I don't want anybody to think there's something going on."

"But there isn't, right?" Nikki quizzed, eyeing Meesa skeptically.

"No, of course not," Meesa laughed trying to play it off. "We're fine. He just couldn't be here today."

"Ok. I'll get right on it then." Nikki rubbed her arm.

"Thank you." Meesa flashed a small smile.

She was so consumed with her marital drama that she'd missed half the show. There were only a few models ahead of Destiny.

"You ready?" She asked, smoothing back Destiny's hair.

"Yeah, I'm about to tear this runway up." Destiny stood up straight and placed her shoulders back.

"I need for you to strut, bitch," Meesa instructed. "Sell the fuckin' gown, ok? Sashay like you're on RuPaul's Drag Race."

"I got it," Destiny winked.

"Ok, go; it's your turn." Meesa pushed her onto the runway.

The crowd began to applaud as soon as she appeared. Meesa could see the look of awe on everyone's face. The gown was magnificent. She watched through the monitor as Destiny switched her hips to the beat. Destiny had one of the best walks in the business. She gave Naomi Campbell a run for her money.

The constant roar of the crowd confirmed that the show was a success. Meesa could finally breathe a sigh of relief. The show was over. It was now time for her and the kids to hit the catwalk.

"You ready, ma?" Kiyan asked taking her hand.

"Yeah," Meesa smiled at her son.

"You did a great job, mommy." Mila took her mother's other hand.

"Thank you, my sweet girl. You ready to hit the runway?"

"Yes." Both kids said in unison.

Meesa and the kids stepped onto the catwalk. Everyone in attendance stood up on their feet and clapped. No matter how many times Meesa did it, tears always welled in her eyes after every show. She never took for granted how blessed she was. She came from nothing. She started from the bottom and now she was at the top of the food chain.

God had blessed her beyond measure. People would die for the life she had. But all that glittered wasn't gold. People thought she was happy but she was dying inside. When things weren't right between her and Black, nothing in her life was right. She couldn't function.

A thousand tears threatened to spill onto her cheeks as she concentrated on not falling apart in front of everyone. Then out of nowhere, she spotted Black out of the corner of her eye. There he was standing off to the side with a bouquet of pink roses. Meesa unknowingly began to smile from ear to ear.

"Mommy, daddy's here!" Mila waved animatedly to her father.

"I see, baby," Meesa smiled and waved too.

Black approached the runway and handed her the flowers.

"Congratulations, baby." He spoke in a low, sexy tone.

Black gave his wife a soft, sweet kiss on the lips. Meesa kissed her husband back. She wanted to punch him in his face but because of the cameras and crowd, she kept her emotions in check. Meesa was over the moon that he was back but she was still upset. She pretended in front of the media that everything between her and Black was good but on the inside she was boiling.

She and the kids took their bow and walked backstage. Meesa couldn't even wrap her brain around the fact that Black had returned before she was accosted by journalist and bloggers. Meesa happily did all of the interviews but her mind was elsewhere. She couldn't wait to talk to Black. As she talked to the press, she searched the backstage area for him with her eyes. It took her a minute to locate him. He was with the kids. They seemed to be relieved as well that their father was home.

It took Meesa two hours to wrap up all of the interviews. The backstage area had cleared out. All of the girls had left to head over to the after party. Nikki took the kids with her so Meesa and Black could have some time alone. Black sat on a stool. One of his feet rested on the rings of the stool while the other sat on the floor. He looked at Meesa. He could tell she was upset.

She had every right to be. He'd behaved childishly. He knew it, but at that moment, Black felt it was best he leave. He needed time to breathe. He would rather burn out than say something he would live to regret. He just wished that Meesa understood him better. They'd been together over ten years. You'd think she would by now.

But sadly, she didn't. Meesa wanted Black to be this white collar, straight laced type of husband. He could never be some wholesome and sweet dude. He was a thug, a hardcore criminal at heart. All he knew was fast money and living dangerously. Life wasn't fun for him if it wasn't on the edge. Living this A-list, Hollywood, mainstream life wasn't for him.

It was fun for a while but after a while the shit became boring. Black had been rich. He knew all the celebrities so none of it meant a thing to him. His name rang bells from East to West. He was considered an OG in the game but Black didn't want to be an afterthought. He wanted the thrill of the hustle again. Overseeing Victor's empire was just what he needed to feel whole again. He just had to find a way to communicate that to Meesa.

Meesa folded her hands across her chest and walked slowly towards him. It was so quiet you could hear their thoughts. As she neared Black, their eyes locked. Meesa hated that he was so goddamn fine. She always lost track of her emotions when placed before him. Black looked devilishly delicious. His locs were freshly washed and twisted. He donned a black Mitchell & Ness snapback, Ray-Ban shades, a Crooks & Castle tee-shirt, a gold chain, Levi blue jean vest, black jeans and Air Yeezy's on his feet.

"So when did you get back?" She asked.

"About an hour ago." Black eyed her lustfully.

"Thanks for the flowers."

"It's nothing. You deserved them. You put on a great show."

"Don't you think that I deserve an apology as well?" Meesa cocked her head to the side.

"Come here." Black said, in a low, raspy tone.

Meesa stood still.

"Come here," he demanded.

Meesa sighed and stepped closer. Black placed his hands on her hips and pulled her in-between his legs.

"I also got you this." He pulled a Harry Winston diamond necklace out of his pocket.

Meesa gasped. The necklace was filled with diamonds.

"You forgive me?"

"Yes," she beamed, putting the necklace on. "But this still don't make up for the fact that you left without me having any way to contact you. That shit wasn't cool, Black. Anything could've happened and I wouldn't have been able to get ahold of you.

"You're right. I was wrong," Black apologized sincerely. "I won't do that again."

"I know the hell you won't," Meesa challenged.

"You forgive me?" Black wrapped his arms around her waist.

His head rested on Meesa's stomach.

"Yeah." She sighed hugging him back.

"Good, 'cause I gotta head back outta town this weekend."

Meesa felt her temperature rise. She was two seconds away from giving him back the necklace and going off. Instead, she held her tongue. If Black was determined to live this street life again, she had to let him do him. When things fell apart he'd only have his self to blame.

PASSIVE AGGRESSIVE
WHEN WE'RE TEXTIN'.
I FEEL THE DISTANCE.
-DRAKE FEAT. JHENE
AIKO, "FROM TIME"

CHAPTER 12

"Mmm… this bacon is so good." Stevie relished the taste of the warm, salty meat. "And these pecan pancakes are fire!"

Gwyn glared at her sister as she ate her breakfast. Stevie was scarfing down her food as if it were her last meal. Gwyn, Stevie and their mom were having breakfast at Cracker Barrel. Gwyn hoped that they would be able to spend the morning together and enjoy each other's company but Stevie was making it very difficult. It was obvious by the sunglasses she wore and her excessive appetite that she was high as a kite.

She wanted to kick Stevie's ass. The fact that she had the balls to go anywhere with them high off weed astonished her. Stevie's little ass didn't have respect for anybody, not even herself. What pissed Gwyn off even more was that her mother sat there oblivious to it all. It was as if her mother had given up. Not only was Stevie high but apparently she'd decided to go out and get a septum ring pierced into her nose.

"So, mama, you allowed Stevie to go get her nose pierced? You signed off on this?" Gwyn questioned, eating a piece of her egg white omelet.

"No, I didn't," Regina responded with an attitude. "She came home with it the other day."

"And you didn't tell her to take it out?"

"No, it's in there now," Regina shrugged.

"How did you even get someone to pierce your nose without mama being there? Don't even answer that. Duh, you used a fake I.D." Gwyn put two and two together.

"Actually, no. I let my friend do it," Stevie giggled .

"And mama you think this is ok?" Gwyn asked vexed.

"Obviously, I don't." Regina rolled her neck.

She was tired of her daughter interrogating her about her mothering skills.

"I yelled at her and put her on punishment for two weeks. Stevie is not to leave the house or go anywhere but school and back."

"So how she get them fresh hickeys on her neck then?" Gwyn pointed with her fork.

Regina whipped her head around and pulled down the collar of Stevie's shirt. Sure enough, there were two, bright red hickeys on the left side of her neck.

"Yo' li'l ass snuck out the house last night didn't you?" Regina quipped.

"Calm down, ma. I only left for a little while." Stevie took a sip of her orange juice as if nothing was wrong.

"So not only are you sitting here high off weed and God knows what else but you snuck out the house and let some li'l boy suck on your neck?" Gwyn snapped.

"Wait a minute, you're high?" Regina asked stunned.

Gwyn rolled her eyes to the sky and groaned.

"Duh, mama, that's why she got on the damn shades so you can't see how red her eyes are," Gwyn replied, feeling sick to her stomach.

Seeing her little sister on such a downward spiral killed Gwyn. She wanted the world for Stevie and worked her butt off to give it to her but Stevie didn't care. She didn't care that she was causing her mother and sister so much pain.

"Oh, when we get home it's on. Yo' ass is getting a whooping," Regina shot pissed.

"Girl, bye." Stevie cracked up laughing.

"Girl, bye? Who she talking too? Mama, I know she ain't talking to you." Gwyn's mouth flew open.

"She's always flipping off at the mouth," Regina spat.

"And you gon' let her talk to you like that?" Gwyn gasped. "When I was her age you would've slapped the piss outta me."

"That's 'cause when you were my age mama could still get around good. She can't run after me with that bad knee," Stevie said sarcastically

"And yo' bad ass takes advantage of it." Gwyn shook her head. "Well guess what? Ain't nothin' wrong with me. I can fuck yo' ass up day or night," Gwyn warned.

"Bye, Felicia." Stevie waved her off.

Gwyn was two seconds away from rearing her hand back and slapping Stevie when she received a text message from Cash.

<Messages   Never Call   Contact

U tryin' to fuck or nah?

In your voice. LOL

Gwyn giggled a little and shook her head. Since that night at the bar, she and Cash hadn't been able to keep their hands off each other. He stayed dicking her down. Their sexual chemistry was off the charts but that's all that she and Cash could ever be. She couldn't allow him further access into her life, although he constantly tried to place himself there.

<Messages   Never Call   Contact

U tryin' to fuck or nah? In your voice. LOL

U silly□… I can't… having breakfast wit' the fam

<Messages   Never Call   Contact

U tryin' to fuck or nah? In your voice. LOL

U silly□… I can't… having breakfast wit' the fam

Where at?

<Messages   Never Call   Contact

U tryin' to fuck or nah? In your voice. LOL

U silly □… I can't… having breakfast wit' the fam

Where at?

Cracker Barrel

<Messages   Never Call   Contact

U tryin' to fuck or nah? In your voice. LOL

U silly□… I can't… having breakfast wit' the fam

Where at?

Cracker Barrel

I'm about to meet u up there

<Messages   Never Call   Contact

U tryin' to fuck or nah? In your voice. LOL

U silly□… I can't… having breakfast wit' the fam

Where at?

Cracker Barrel

I'm about to meet u up there

U don't have to

Five minutes later, after no response, Gwyn texted him again and said:

Really... u don't have to come.

I'll get up with u later.

Ten minutes passed by and Cash still didn't reply back. Gwyn's palms began to sweat. She'd only allowed one man to meet her family and that was Trey. After their relationship ended, she vowed to never let anyone she dated meet them unless she had a ring on her finger. She liked Cash a lot but he was overstepping his boundaries by constantly forcing himself on her. Gwyn looked around the restaurant nervously in search of him.

"What's wrong wit' you?" Stevie asked picking up on her nervousness.

"Nothing," Gwyn lied. "Eat your food and mind your business. As a matter-of-fact, are y'all done eating 'cause I'm about to ask for the check?"

"No. We just got our food." Regina looked at Gwyn as if she were crazy.

Then it happened. Gwyn heard a young girl shriek.

"Oh my God it's Cash!"

Everyone in the restaurant spun around in their seats to get a good view of him. People pulled out their phones and snapped pictures of him as he came her way.

"Jesus be a fence! It's Cash!" Stevie lost her mind. "O M muthafuckin' G, he's coming our way!" She took off her glasses.

"Sister, how do I look?" Stevie fixed her hair and sat up straight.

"You look fine." Gwyn screwed up her face.

She didn't have the time or the patience for Stevie's li'l hot ass to be fawning over Cash. She had bigger fish to fry, like how she was going to get Cash out of there.

"What's up, beautiful?" He leaned down and kissed her cheek.

"Hi."

"Sister, you know Cash and didn't even tell me?" Stevie popped her lips.

"It's a lot of things I don't tell you," Gwyn replied. "What are you doing here?" She stood up and hugged Cash.

"I told you not to come."

"You did? I ain't get that message," Cash blatantly lied. "Introduce me to the fam."

Gwyn rolled her eyes so hard she thought they were going to fall out. She was nervous as hell. It didn't help that the whole entire restaurant was focused on them. This was exactly what she didn't want.

"Cash, this is my mother, Regina, and my little sister Stevie," Gwen replied nervously.

"Nice to meet you, ma'am." Cash reached out his hand to give Regina a handshake.

"Nice to meet you too, dear." Regina shook his hand.

She had no idea that she was shaking hands with her daughter's baby's father.

"You ain't tell me that you had such a pretty little sister," Cash said to Gwyn.

"I like to keep my personal life private. So now that you've met everyone, you can go now." She tried to push him towards the door.

"Sister, stop being so rude," Stevie remarked.

"Yeah, you trippin'. I'm about to eat and, Stevie, it's a pleasure to meet you as well." Cash shook her hand.

He couldn't help but notice that she and Gwyn were damn near identical twins.

"The pleasure is all mine." Stevie eyed him hungrily.

Cash took a seat next to Gwyn and ordered his food. After his order was placed, he made small talk with the ladies.

"So how long have you been knowing my sister?" Stevie asked while toying with her straw with her tongue.

"Believe it or not, since '99. We met then and lost touch. We just recently linked back up."

"That's what's up. So y'all dating, hooking up, boyfriend and girlfriend? What's up? Let a sister know."

"Umm… that's none of your business, li'l girl," Gwyn snapped.

"Yeah, stay in a child's place, Stevie," Regina reprimanded her.

"I'm far from a child. I'm fourteen going on fifteen. Ain't nothing little about me." Stevie stressed, poking her chest out.

Cash caught her flirtatious advances and quickly looked away.

"Now do you see why I didn't want you to come?" Gwyn said loud enough that only he could hear.

"It's cool; she's young. She don't know no better."

"That's what I keep telling myself," Gwyn replied, praying Cash couldn't hear the sound of her rapidly beating heart.

Having him there with her family was going to give her a heart attack. This was something she never planned for or wanted. She had to end this breakfast date quick.

"Has anyone ever told you two that you look like twins?" Cash asked still blown away by Gwyn and Stevie's strong resemblance to one another.

"I don't think they look alike at all," Regina spoke up. "I think Stevie looks just like me."

"Me too," Gwyn agreed.

"I hear it all the time but I think I look better than Gwyn. Don't you agree?" Stevie winked her eye at Cash.

"Lord, take me now!" Gwyn looked to heaven for guidance.

An hour later, the disastrous breakfast date was over. Gwyn couldn't have been happier. She damn near ran out of the restaurant. She was beyond ready to go. She would've exploded if she had to sit there any longer. Stevie was in rare form. Gwyn had never seen her little sister behave that way. She soon realized that if you placed a fine man with some paper in front of her, Stevie was TTG: trained to go.

Homegirl had no shame in her game at all. Stevie was worse off than Gwyn thought. She and her mother were going to have to do some sort of intervention, and quick. Gwyn, Cash, Regina and Stevie filed out of the restaurant. The late morning breeze kissed each of their skin. Gwyn stood to the side as Cash signed autographs and took pictures. She loved to see how sweet he was with his fans.

"Gwyn, give me the keys so me and Stevie can go sit in the car," Regina requested, holding out her hand.

Gwyn handed her mother the keys.

"Cash, it was nice meeting you and thanks for breakfast."

"It was my pleasure." He kissed her on the cheek.

"Gwyn, I like him. He's a keeper," Regina tapped her daughter on the leg.

"I'm sure you do," Gwyn mumbled.

Her mother was completely oblivious to the fact that she'd just shared a meal with the man that had impregnated her daughter years before. Regina was in the dark and Gwyn planned on keeping it that way. There was no sense in dredging up the past. Besides, this would be the first and last time she or Stevie would ever see Cash again.

"Thanks for breakfast, Cash." Stevie wrapped her arms around his neck, pressed her breasts up against his chest and hugged him tight. "I hope you got all you could eat."

"Get yo' ass in the car!" Gwyn yanked her off of him and pushed her towards the car.

Stevie stumbled a bit but caught her footing and walked away as told.

"I don't know what I'm going to do with that li'l girl." Gwyn massaged her temples.

"Yeah, she is a wild one. Kinda like somebody else I know," Cash teased.

"That's not a good thing. I don't want her to be anything like me," Gwyn said seriously.

"Why not? You're a success. You went from dancing to helping run a billion dollar company."

"Yeah but I made a lot of mistakes along the way. Some that still haunt me to this day." Gwyn stared off into space.

She thought of the baby that she'd given up for adoption.

"Look, I apologize for always being so distant but—"

"No more buts," Cash cut her off. "If you're really sorry make it up to me later by having dinner with me."

Gwyn swallowed hard. She wanted to say no but the puppy dog face Cash was giving her was simply irresistible.

"Ok." She lied instead. "I'll call you later so we can set up a time."

ALL YOU SEE IS ASS.
-CHRISS ZOE FEAT. AV,
"CUT UP"

CHAPTER 13

The Coliseum was packed to capacity. Everybody that was somebody was at the place. Drinks flowed and the dance floor was filled. Black stood posted up in the V.I.P section with his crew. A bevy of women surrounded him but one female stood out the most. It was the birthday girl, Brandy. Baby girl was rocking the hell out of the baby pink Herve Leger dress he'd given her money to buy earlier in the week.

It was money well spent. The dress clung to her body like glue. Brandy looked good as fuck. Years of stripping had done her body good. She had a sick, toned, fit physique. Her 38 DD breast implants and silicone enhanced ass gave her a Kim Kardashian appeal. The ombre, black and honey blonde, Cambodian weave she rocked reached all the way down to her butt.

Brandy swung her weave from left to right as she shook her ass to the beat of Laudie's *Stripper Bop*. Black loved to see her twerk. Brandy knew how to move her body like no other. She was a hot girl. She stayed laced in the illest, most expensive designer pieces. Brandy kept her hair, makeup, nails and feet on point. Diamonds dripped from her neck, wrist and ears. She was a bad bitch and she knew it

For years Black kept his distance. He had been a happily married man. But when he and Meesa started having problems, old habits reemerged. Black threw caution to the wind. He started to do him. When he ran into Brandy while on a trip to Vegas, the two reconnected and began hooking up. Brandy was fun. She didn't try to change him. She allowed him to be who he was.

They always turned up when together. Brandy liked to do all of the things Black liked to do. She liked to drink, smoke, talk shit and hit the club. Meesa used to be down but now all she cared about was photo shoots, dressing celebrities and staying in the press. Anything that would disturb her goody two-shoes reputation was off limits.

Meesa wasn't fun anymore. He still loved her dearly but she was boring and stuffy. All she did was bitch and complain. Brandy hardly ever had anything negative to say. She had her own life so she wasn't so concerned with his. She was a former stripper turned pole dance instructor and mother of one. Brandy had multiple dudes that she kicked it with but Black was by far her favorite. He kicked her down dough and good dick. Nothing about her changed. She still didn't give a fuck about anything but herself.

"Y'all having a good time tonight?" DJ Needles asked into the microphone.

The crowd roared.

"Ok, it's time for birthday shout-outs. I wanna give a birthday shout-out to the birthday girl, Brandy! You lookin' good tonight, baby!"

"Thank you, baby!" Brandy held up her glass of champagne. "And thank you, baby." She turned and planted a deep, sensual kiss on Black's lips.

"I love my outfit."

"I told you, I got you." Black rubbed her ass.

"You always got me, baby." Brandy kissed him again.

Black didn't even stop her. He'd been cheating for the past year and hadn't got caught. He felt invincible. Meesa didn't know anything about Brandy and he planned on keeping it that way. There was no way he was going to lose his wife.

"I can't wait to get you out of here tonight," Brandy purred, massaging his dick through his pants.

"Oh word? What you gon' do?"

Before Brandy could respond, Black's cell phone vibrated. Black released Brandy from his grasp and pulled his phone out his pocket. To his surprise, it was Meesa. Meesa was never up at that time of night. It was 3:00am in New York. Black's heart began to race. He hoped there wasn't anything wrong with the kids.

"Hold up. I gotta take this. It's my wife." He stepped off to the side.

Brandy eyed him with disdain and sucked her teeth. She tried to pretend like she didn't care that Meesa was a priority over her but secretly she did. She hated playing second fiddle to her. It had been that way since they were younger. She figured that being as uncomplicated as possible would make Black catch feelings for her but it didn't. He was madly in love with Meesa. Brandy understood that she was his wife but tonight was all about her. Black could put her ass on the back burner for one night.

"Hello?" Black yelled into the phone.

"I was just calling to tell you goodnight. Where are you?"

"At the Coliseum," Black replied truthfully.

He knew that Meesa didn't keep up with anything that had to do with St. Louis.

"When are you coming home? We miss you."

"I miss you and the kids too. I'll be home Monday."

"Oh ok…" Meesa held the phone. "Well call me when you get back to your room."

"You'll be sleep, babe," Black laughed.

"Just do it please," Meesa insisted.

Something didn't feel right in her spirit. She could almost sense that Black was up to no good.

"A'ight, have a goodnight." Black ended the call.

He had no intentions on calling Meesa when he got to his room. He'd be doing other things when he got there. Black placed his phone back inside his pocket and found Brandy sitting on the couch with her arms akimbo and her legs crossed. Homegirl had a serious, stank look plastered on her face.

"What's wrong wit' you?" Black lifted her up onto her feet.

"You said today was going to be all about me." Brandy poked out her bottom lip.

"And it is. Didn't I buy you this outfit? Didn't I buy out the bar? Aren't we flying to Chicago in the morning to go shopping?"

"Yeah," she pouted.

"So what you trippin' for?"

"It just irks me sometimes when she interrupts our time together, baby." Brandy traced her finger across his chest.

"Chill out. That's my wife. I'ma always answer the phone when she calls."

Brandy rolled her eyes. She had to remind herself that she was Black's side bitch. She wasn't going to dare catch feelings for him again.

"Whatever. I don't even care. I don't wanna talk about that shit no more. I wanna dance." She turned around and backed her ass up on him.

Black took a shot of tequila to the head and watched her do her thing.

Kelly couldn't get out of the house fast enough to see Dre. Since their steamy encounter at the park, they'd been kicking it non-stop. She couldn't get him off her mind. She thought about him night and day. Visions of his face invaded her thoughts when she tried to concentrate on work. When she was with her son she found herself reminiscing on the feel of his tongue. When she showered she touched herself just so she could pretend like she was with him.

She imagined that her fingers were his tongue on her clit. Kelly hadn't been this sexually aroused in years. Jaden had never brought out this side of her. When they had sex he was strictly a missionary position man. For years, Kelly had nothing to compare his sex game to but now that she did, there was no way she was going back.

All week long she'd counted down the days till she saw Dre again. It was finally the weekend. She was meeting up with him at Greenhouse that night. Kelly had received a full makeover earlier that day. She wanted to look her absolute best. Kelly flew in celebrity hairstylist, Larry Sims, and makeup artist, Renny Vasquez, to do her hair and beat her face.

Kelly had decided to get rid of her locs and go back straight. Larry was able to comb them out and give her a sleek hairdo. Her natural hair reached down to the middle of her back. Renny gave her a dramatic smokey eye and a bold, cherry red lip. Celebrity stylist, Farrah James, hooked her up with a banging Miss A strapless dress. The dress was sculpted and figure-hugging. Pleated panels framed a cutout bodice.

Kelly felt sexy and confident. She hadn't felt this self-assured since she was a teenager and it was all because of Dre. His constant affirmations of her beauty made her feel special. For the first time in her life she was making herself happy and it felt amazing. She'd left Jaden Jr. at home with his father so she could go out. Jaden wasn't too pleased with having to watch his son on the weekend.

That was normally his time to kick it but he complied. Kelly not kicking him down any dough was killing him. He figured the more accommodating he was, the quicker she would be to forgive him. Kelly, on the other hand, hadn't even thought about forgiving Jaden. As a matter-of-fact, he was the furthest thing from her mind. She could care less about his well-being. Her mind was consumed with Dre.

Kelly tugged on the bottom of her skirt as she walked into the club. She looked great but was totally uncomfortable with the barely there outfit. She'd never shown that much skin before. Her tits were out for the world to see. She felt like all eyes were on her, which they were. Kelly's body was banging.

Dre spotted her as soon as she walked in. His jaw dropped open as soon as he laid eyes on her. Kelly had gone all out. She'd totally changed her entire look. Dre was happy to see her go to such an extreme level just to please him. He welcomed her with open arms.

"Damn, baby, you look good as fuck." He kissed her lips intensely.

"You like it for real?" Kelly asked coming up for air. "I don't look slutty, do I?"

"No, you look sexy as fuck. Here." He reached for her hand and placed it on his hard dick. "That's how good you look."

Kelly began to massage his bulge through his pants.

"Keep that up and I'ma take you in the bathroom and get a taste." Dre sniffed, palming her ass.

"You gon' let me get a taste?" He palmed her ass and aggressively kissed her on the mouth.

Kelly loved when he kissed her forcefully. The intensity of his kisses turned her on to the fullest.

"Mmm," she moaned. "Baby, I missed you."

"I missed you too." Dre hungrily licked her neck.

Kelly didn't care that there were other people around watching them. She was completely caught up in the moment. The music was pounding, lights were flashing and she was in sexual overdrive. For once, she was letting go and being free.

"Ay yo', I want to introduce you to my peoples." Dre abruptly stopped kissing her and led her over to his table. "These are my boys, Eric and Rico."

"Hi." Kelly waved.

"You thirsty? You want something to drink?" Dre asked handing her a bottle of Ace of Spades.

"Yeah." Kelly took the bottle and held it.

She naturally assumed that he would hand her a glass but he didn't.

"What you waiting for? Drink up!" Dre took a bottle to the head. "Whew! Yeah!"

Kelly giggled. She was utterly mesmerized by how carefree he was. She wanted to be just like him so she decided to throw caution to the wind and guzzled down the alcohol.

"That a girl." Dre whisked her out onto the dance floor.

Wiz Khalifa's summer anthem *Ass Drop* bumped loud. Buzzed, Kelly did exactly what the song said and dropped down low to the floor. She hadn't dropped it down on a man since Juvenile came out with *Back That Thang Up*. Kelly normally hated nightclubs but tonight was different. She was having the time of her life.

Dre never gave her the opportunity to think. With him, everything was spur-of-the-moment. Kelly swung her head from side-to-side. She was busting out dance moves she didn't even know she had. Dre tried his best to keep up with her but he couldn't. His high was coming down and he needed a pick me up. Dre reached inside his suit jacket and pulled out a small bottle of cocaine. Kelly was oblivious to what he was doing until she saw him a place a thin wand up to his nose and inhale.

"You want some?" Dre asked casually.

"No," she refused. "I haven't done blow in over ten years. I'm good."

"C'mon, kick it wit' me." He placed the wand in front of her face.

Kelly rolled her eyes to the ceiling. She really didn't want to do blow but didn't want to come across as a bore. Reluctantly, she leaned forward and sniffed the coke. Immediately, she felt a rush of adrenaline shoot through her body. Kelly could feel her feet levitate off the floor. She was experiencing euphoria. Her entire body was tingling. She'd forgotten how good cocaine made her feel. *Why did I ever stop doing this,* she thought unable to feel her face.

GON' AND LAY YO'
HEAD BACK WHILE I
SET IT OFF.
-BRANDY, "DO YOU
KNOW WHAT YOU
HAVE"

CHAPTER 14

It was a gorgeous afternoon. The sun was shining brightly. It was 65 degrees outside. Fall was right around the corner. Meesa was determined to soak up the last few days of summer. She and the girls sat in the center of Jean-Gorges restaurant. Jean-Gorges was one of Meesa's favorite places to go dine. Since opening in 1997, Jean-Gorges offered the best French, American and Asian influenced dishes.

What set the experience off even more was the immaculate décor and design. White walls, huge windows, white chiffon drapes, white table clothes and neutral colored chairs gave the restaurant and open, airy feel. Everything was clean and pristine just how Meesa liked it. She and the girls were dressed to the nine in designer duds.

Kelly wore Prada. Gwyn rocked Versace. Nikki looked elegant and classy in Catherine Malandrino. Destiny showed off her long, lean legs in Rodarte. Meesa was laced in head to toe Alexander McQueen. All of the ladies looked fabulous. Meesa truly enjoyed when they all could come together to enjoy a great meal, gossip and catch up on each others lives.

"Ya'll, I don't know what me and my mama gon' do with Stevie," Gwyn began. "That child is out of control."

"She acts just like you," Kelly snorted with laughter.

"Bye Felicia." Gwyn flicked her off. "That's what I'm trying to prevent."

"Stevie is bad as hell," Nikki chimed in.

"Let me know when it's two o'clock, Nikki," Meesa said. "I gotta go pick Black up from the airport."

"Ok," she nodded.

"Ahhhhhhhh I am so tired," Destiny yawned.

"From what? You don't do shit," Gwyn teased.

"Lies you tell. Honey, I was up all night riding that surfboard. Let me tell you something. She, me, her experienced major back breakage last night. Ya' feel me. My baby put it down."

"Ugh enough," Meesa turned up her nose. "I am trying to eat and quiet down. Other people can hear you. "

"See, that's your problem. You act too bougie for me." Destiny waved her off.

"No, I don't." Meesa gasped, placing her hand on her chest.

"I'm sorry, friend but I agree," Nikki chimed in.

Meesa knew that there must be some truth to Destiny's words if Nikki agreed. Nikki was the sweet quiet one.

"I don't feel like I'm bougie," Meesa frowned.

"Well, you are. You're stuffy as hell now. You don't ever turn loose no more. You're just... blah. You're just there," Destiny scowled.

"Well damn, tell me how you really feel."

"No tea, no shade. We just speaking the truth. Black ain't never told you that?"

Meesa thought back on all the times Black confided in her that she needed to unwind and get back to her roots. She never paid him any mind because she felt it was just an excuse for him to be on some hood shit.

"Yeah, he has." She fessed up. "I just blew him off."

"Well, bitch you need to listen. I want the old Meesa back," Destiny continued.

"You heffa's better leave my friend alone." Kelly hugged Meesa from the side. "I think you're fine just the way you are, friend."

"Thank you," Meesa flashed her megawatt smile.

"I think she's great too but the bitch still needs to loosen the fuck up," Destiny declared.

"What are you over there doing?" Nikki asked Gwyn noticing how quiet she was.

"I'm on Instagram going through my friend Peaches pictures. We used to strip together."

"Don't remind us," Meesa sighed.

"See," Destiny pointed. "That's what I'm talking about."

"Yeah, 'cause while you sighing you need to let me teach you some of my old dance moves." Gwyn checked her.

"I have always wanted to learn how to make my booty clap." Meesa snickered like a little school girl.

"We can take one of Brandy's pole dancing classes. You know she's a pole instructor now."

"Don't bring up that bitch name to me. I haven't thought about her in years." Meesa's nostrils flared.

"Uh oh," Destiny leaned back. "There go ghetto Meesa."

"Shut up," Meesa laughed.

"So Peaches was at Brandy's birthday party Friday night," Gwyn spoke out loud to herself.

"How you know?"

"Cause they're on a picture together and Peaches tagged Brandy in it."

"Mmm," Meesa mumbled irritated by the sound of Brandy's name.

Although it had been over ten years since her drama with Brandy, Meesa still couldn't stand her. The bitch was a parasite. Meesa was happy that she was out of her life.

"Brandy looks cute. She has a lot of work done but cute none the less."

"Let me see," Destiny reached her hand out for Gwyn's phone.

Gwyn handed it to her.

"Yeah the bitch is aging well. Meesa, you wanna see." Destiny shoved the phone in her face.

"If you don't get that shit away from me," Meesa warned heated.

"What? I thought you would want to see your best friend," Destiny giggled. "I'm getting ready to go on her page."

"Don't accidently like one of her pics, lil' dumb ass girl," Gwyn sneered.

"I'm not." Destiny waved her off and proceeded to click on Brandy's IG page.

Her IG name was WhenYoNiggaWantMe. Destiny clicked on Brandy's last post which was from that morning. It was a picture of her lying naked in bed wrapped up in a set of sheets. Her head was lying on an unidentified man's chest. The dudes arm was draped around her neck. Destiny's heart stopped beating causing her to nearly drop Gwyn's phone in her soup.

"Girl, you bet not drop my phone! What's wrong wit' you?" Gwyn screeched.

"Look." Destiny handed Gwyn her phone back.

Gwyn examined the picture and all of the color in her face left.

"What is wrong with ya'll?" Nikki asked confused.

"Meesa, sweetie, you might wanna take a look at this." Gwyn passed her the phone.

Meesa looked at the picture. It was the first time in years she'd seen her arch nemesis' face. Her stomach instantly began to churn but it wasn't Brandy that was making her sick. It was the man's arm that was wrapped around her. The man was dark skin with a picture of Jesus' face tattooed on his forearm. It was the same tattoo Black had on his arm. Tears filled Meesa's throat.

She wanted to cry but she couldn't. She had to save face in front of her friends. Besides, the picture location said Chicago, Illinois. Black was in St. Louis so it couldn't have been him. At least that's what she was going to tell her friends. Meesa handed Gwyn back her phone.

"Chile, that ain't Black, He's in St. Louis. That picture was taken in Chicago."

"Meesa, that's Black's arm." Gwyn looked at her in disbelief.

"It's not Black, ok. I think I would know how my husband's arm looks." Meesa countered with an attitude. "There are a million dudes that are dark skin with Jesus tattoos. That ain't Black. He would never cheat on me with that bitch again."

"Ok," Gwyn shrugged. "If you say so."

"I do, so drop it."

Meesa couldn't get to the airport fast enough. The entire ride over she kept envisioning the picture in her mind. She could deny it to her friends until she was blue in the face but she couldn't deny it to herself. The man in the picture was Black. She knew every crevice and fold of his entire body. She'd examined and explored it for years.

He'd wrapped that same arm around her a million times throughout the years.

That same arm had held her when she needed a shoulder to cry on, when they made love, when she fell asleep at night and when she was afraid. It broke her heart that he would hold another woman the same way he held her. It hurt to the core to know that the woman was Brandy. In the beginning of their relationship, Black's affair with Brandy had caused Meesa pain.

To know that he would so selfishly go there again knowing that it would emotionally kill her was soul crushing. Meesa wanted to hate Brandy because she knew that they were married. But she wasn't married to Brandy. She was married to Black. He was the one who promised to love, respect and be faithful to her and she was the one who had believed him. She was the one who trusted him whole heartedly with every fiber of her being.

Meesa gripped the steering wheel and tried to focus on the road. She could barely drive and think straight. Her eyes were flooded with tears. Her whole entire world had shattered. She knew that she and Black were going through a rough patch but never did she think it would cause him to fall into another woman's arms.

"How could he do this to me?" She asked herself out loud.

Tears poured from her eyes.

"Why would he sleep with that bitch again? Why, god? Why?" Meesa cried.

She'd told him ten years prior that if he ever cheated on her again she would be out the door. Did he think it was a game? Did he not believe her when she said it? There was no way she could stay with him knowing that he'd betrayed her trust with the same woman he'd betrayed her trust with before. It was obvious that they had some type of connection. Maybe he loved her.

Meesa felt like she was suffocating. She couldn't handle the pain she was feeling. She didn't even know if she would have the strength to confront him. Meesa could barely breathe. Through the will of god she made it to the airport pick-up station. Black was standing front and center. He waved at Meesa. Meesa didn't bother waving back. She pulled up to the curb and popped the trunk. Black put his things in the trunk and got in.

"What's up, baby?" He reached over to give her a kiss.

Meesa jerked back and said, "Don't touch me."

"What's wrong wit' you?" Black asked noticing that her eyes were blood shot red with tears.

"Baby, what's wrong? What happened? Are the kids ok?" He panicked. "Is my dad ok?"

"Everybody's fine." Meesa reached across him and opened the glove compartment.

She found a box of tissues, took a few out and blew her nose.

"What's the matter then?"

Instead of responding Meesa pulled out her phone and went to Instagram. She went on Brandy's page and clicked on the picture.

"Is this you?" She held up the phone. "Are you cheating on me again with Brandy?"

Black looked at the picture. His whole entire body went numb. *I told that bitch not to post that picture,* he thought.

"What?" He leaned his head back on the headrest. "Are you fuckin' serious? Fuck nah, that ain't me," he lied.

"So I'm crazy, huh? That ain't your arm, Black?"

"Nooooo, man," Black responded angrily. "What the fuck are you talkin' about? I was in St. Louis. That picture was taken in Chicago. Look, I ain't come home for this shit. Ain't nobody got time for you to be accusing me of a bunch of dumb shit. I could've stayed in St. Louis if I knew this was what I was going to come home to."

"If it ain't you then what you getting mad for?" Meesa shot. "What you getting amped for?"

"'Cause, let you tell it, I'm always up to know good. We've been married for how many years now and you still don't trust me?" He screwed up his face.

"You damn right, I don't trust you 'cause I know this is you." Meesa took the car out of park and pulled off.

"A'ight it's me," Black shot back sarcastically. "I was in Chicago fuckin' another bitch."

"Think it's a game, Black. I will pack up me and my kids so fast—"

"You can leave but you ain't taking my kids no muthafuckin' where," Black barked. "You get on my nerves with always trying to threaten me. You gon' stop that shit."

"When we get home, move your shit into the guest room."

"That's cool." Black shrugged not giving a fuck. "Anything else you want, your highness?"

Meesa continued to drive. There was no point in going back and forth with him. He was never going to admit the truth. Black was still the same manipulative liar he always was. Meesa just had to prove it.

I'M STILL LOST AND
YOU'RE STILL FINE.
-BEYONCÉ FEAT.
DRAKE, "MINE"

CHAPTER 15

For a random Monday night, the gym in Gwyn's building was full. Gwyn focused on the television screen before her as she ran at top speed on the treadmill. She'd been running for what seemed like hours. So many thoughts plagued her mind that she wanted to run forever. She wanted to run to the edge of the earth. At least then she'd be alone. With all of the stress in her life, she wanted nothing more than to escape.

For the last few weeks she'd been staying at the Waldorf Astoria Hotel just to avoid running into Cash but now she was back home. After the unexpected breakfast date from hell, she had to escape. Cash was getting way too close for comfort and Stevie's ratchet behavior was driving Gwyn up the wall. She was at her wits end. She hated the fact that she lied to Cash about seeing him later that night but she had to do what she had to do.

Cash could never be anything more than a fuck buddy. Their past had already messed up any kind of possible future they could ever have. But as Gwyn ran harder and faster on the treadmill, thoughts of his smile, the way he caressed her skin when they made love, his excitement to know her hopes and dreams made her smile.

Cash was more than a rapper. He was a gentle and sweet guy. When in her presence, he always tried to make her feel special and at ease. Cash didn't deserve to be treated like a bug-a-boo or a scrub. There were plenty of women dying to be with him. Gwyn just wasn't one of them. She knew how to push her feelings aside.

Cash had called a few times since breakfast but Gwyn dodged each of his calls. She figured silence was best. He'd eventually get the picture and move on, which it seemed he had. Gwyn wished that she could tell him her secret but revealing the fact that they had a child out in the world would only complicate things. Revealing the secret would devastate too many lives. Either Cash was going to learn to accept Gwyn's limitations or she would cut off all communication with him at once.

Gwyn slowed the speed down on the treadmill. Sweat poured from her body. Since returning home to her building, Gwyn had done a phenomenal job of avoiding Cash. Instead of taking the elevator, she took the stairs. Instead of parking in the garage, she parked outside on the lot. She didn't even come straight home from work because

Cash knew what time she got off. Instead, Gwyn would go to one of the girls' house or out shopping. She did whatever she could to avoid him but Gwyn couldn't avoid Cash for long.

Surprisingly, her iPhone beeped several times alerting her that he was trying to FaceTime her. Gwyn took a quick sip of water and wondered should she answer it. After a while, she figured why the hell not. She was going to have to face him one day. Gwyn placed on her earphones, pressed accept and waited for Cash's face to appear.

"Hello?" She said walking now instead of running on the treadmill.

"What you doing?" Cash gazed into the screen as he smoked a blunt.

"Working out. What you doing?" Gwyn panted.

"In the studio." Cash panned the camera around the room so she could see.

"Sounds like fun. What you working on?" Gwyn made small talk.

"C'mon, man, let's cut the bullshit. Why you keep ducking and dodging a nigga like I'm one of these lame-ass dudes out here? Like I'm some wack-ass nigga or something. I've been seeing you creep in and out the building like a psycho."

"Shut up." Gwyn hung her head in embarrassment.

"Ok, so I'm a liar too? Ok, I see how you do," Cash said with a laugh. "You be on some bullshit, Gwyn, and you know it. Look, you and I both know that I'm digging the fuck outta you. I really wanna see where this can go but you gotta give me some kind of incentive 'cause right now you got me hanging on a limb. I mean, if you want me to fall back, I will. Just let a nigga know what's up."

Gwyn inhaled deep then exhaled. She'd rehearsed this moment over and over again in her mind. She knew it was coming but now that the moment was here and she and Cash were face to face, she couldn't tell him that she never wanted to see him again. It would be a lie. She could never look into his beautiful, brown eyes and tell him to leave her life. There was already too many emotions involved. This was why she had been avoiding him. She knew that whenever she was in Cash's presence that she would become weak. He was her kryptonite.

"Cat got ya' tongue, nigga?" He teased.

"Nah, I'm just soaking in everything you said." Gwyn replied, turning off the treadmill so she could catch her breath.

She found a deserted corner of the gym and sat down on a bench before she continued speaking. Gwyn chose her words carefully.

"I like you, Cash, a lot. Probably more than you know," she confessed. "I just can't afford to open myself up to you and then get hurt, which I know is going to happen."

"See, there you go jumping to conclusions. Who said I was gonna hurt you? Hell, you might fuck around and hurt me."

"And I'm afraid of that too. That's why I keep my distance."

"Man, stop it." Cash leaned back in his chair. "Keeping yo' distance for what? I done been all up in that shit. Ain't no keeping no distance. You're mine whether you wanna be or not. So listen, later on this week me and you gon' go out. I got something special planned, a'ight?"

"Ok." Gwyn gave in.

"No running away this time. I'm done playing games wit' you, Gwyn," Cash declared seriously.

"Ok, daddy," Gwyn said in a ghetto girl tone.

"You stupid," Cash chuckled. "I'ma hit you later; answer the fuckin' phone, Gwyn. I don't wanna have to fuck you up."

"Ok-ok-ok," she grinned giddily.

Across town Kelly stood helplessly. She hung off Dre's every word as he spoke.

"Lay on your stomach," he demanded.

Kelly gazed into his eyes and did exactly as she was told. In the center of his living room was a small, wooden bench with arm restraints attached to it. Kelly lay on top of it. Her arms dangled off one end while her legs hung off the back. Dre happily took her hands and cuffed them to the bottom of the bench. All of the lights were off. The soft flicker of light from strategically placed candles lit the room. Kelly wore no bra, just a black G-string, fishnet stockings and heels.

"Spread your legs opens." Dre commanded eyeing her lustfully.

Kelly slowly spread her legs wide.

"What next?"

"Did I tell you to speak?" He hit her on the butt with a slender impulse crop.

"I'm sorry, daddy!" Kelly whimpered.

"Shut up!" Dre shouted putting a ball gag in her mouth. "I told you not to speak." He licked the side of her face.

"I'm sorry," Kelly mumbled enjoying every second.

Before Dre she'd never experience bondage but ever since he'd introduced her to the art form she loved it. She never thought that she would get off on being restrained and dominated but the shit enticed her. Dre's commanding presence and torture of her body took her to unexpected heights of ecstasy. Bondage, along with cocaine, was a lethal combination.

Kelly couldn't get enough of either one. She found herself craving both all the time. Unbeknownst to her, she'd picked up quite a habit. She spent so much time with Dre getting high and fucking that she barely ever went home. She only went home to check on her son and change her clothes; then she was back out the door again.

She caught the evil looks Jaden shot her when she did go home but Kelly didn't give a damn about what Jaden thought. She was doing her like he'd been doing him for years. It was high time she made herself happy for once 'cause he for damn sure wasn't going to be the one to make her happy.

"You ready to behave now?" Dre sat in front of her face.

"Mmm hmm," Kelly nodded her head profusely.

"You better not say a fuckin' word." He removed the ball gag form her mouth.

"I'm sorry, daddy. Forgive me please," Kelly pleaded.

"There you go being hardheaded!" Dre yanked her head back by her hair. "Now I'ma have to punish you."

Dre stood up and turned the video camera on. Kelly examined the red dot as it lit up. She knew he was filming her but she was too high and caught up in the moment to protest. Dre unzipped his pants and pulled his dick out. His thick, ten inches of man meat dangled in front of Kelly's face.

"Suck it."

Kelly licked her lips and took all of him in her mouth. As she devoured Dre's dick with her tongue, Rico came up from behind and inserted his self deep within her walls. Kelly moaned and relished the feeling of him pounding in and out of her while she sucked Dre's dick. No other feeling could compare to how she felt at that moment. She wanted it again and again. Kelly would give her all to savor the feeling.

MY HEADS UNDER
WATER BUT I'M
BREATHING FINE.
-JOHN LEGEND, "ALL
OF ME"

CHAPTER 16

Black sat in his man cave smoking a Cuban cigar and drinking Peach infused Ciroc. The weight of the world was on his shoulders. Meesa was on to him. He'd been so careful at hiding his affair. Black never once slipped up or so he thought. He knew that he had no business fucking back around with Brandy.

The chick was nothing but trouble but she was also a damn good time. The things Black couldn't do with Meesa, he could do with her. Meesa was too busy trying to uphold her All- American, good girl image. Black missed the old Meesa. The old Meesa was adventurous and carefree.

The new, judgmental and controlling Meesa was a damn headache. Black wanted that old thing back. He missed the way she used to adore him and hang onto his every word. Now Meesa acted like she barely needed him. Black didn't know what to do. Meesa wasn't a dummy. She knew that was him on the picture.

It was only a matter of time before the shit hit the fan. Black had fucked up royally. He'd played with fire and soon he would be burned. Before the truth came out, he had to end things with Brandy. The last year had been fun but keeping his wife and kids was far more important. Black made sure the coast was clear. It was. Meesa was upstairs watching a movie with the kids. Black picked up the phone and dialed Brandy's number.

"Hey, baby," she answered sweetly.

"What you doing? Did I catch you at a bad time?" Black quizzed.

"Kinda, I'm about to teach another class. Why? What's up?"

"Yo', we need to talk."

"About what?"

"We gon' have to chill out," Black stressed.

"Chill out for what, a minute or for good?" Brandy said confused.

"For good? Meesa saw that picture that I told you not to post on Instagram and flipped."

"Oh my bad," Brandy grinned devilishly. "I didn't think it would be a big deal if I posted it but umm, ok. If that's what you want then cool."

She honestly didn't care if Black cut things off with her. Brandy had a plethora of men in her back pocket. Besides that, in a few years Black would get tired of Meesa and come running back to her, again.

"Ain't no other pics of me on there is it?" Black asked nervously.

"Nah, you good."

"A'ight then. You be good."

"Yep." Brandy hung up.

Pleased with himself, Black took a sip of his drink. All he had to do now was stick to his story and convince Meesa that he was telling the truth, which he wasn't. As Black took another swig of his drink, he heard a soft tap on the door. He looked over his shoulder and found his father. Black felt bad. Between flying back and forth from New York to St. Louis, overseeing a half a billion dollar drug empire and juggling two women Black barely had anytime to spend with his father.

"You ain't gotta knock, Pop. Come on in."

Ron came in and closed the door behind him.

"I didn't want to interrupt your phone call."

"So you heard my conversation?" Black asked as he poured his father a glass of ginger ale.

Ron no longer drank alcohol.

"Unfortunately, yes." Ron sat at the bar and intertwined his fingers. "You know I try to stay out of grown folks business but, son, I gotta say this because if I don't my spirit ain't gon' be right."

"Say what's on your mind Pop." Black sat across from him.

"I'm happy you told that gal you was fooling around with that it's over. That was the right thing to do but you just like I overheard you, Meesa could have too. You gots to be more careful, son. You have a good girl up there. That woman loves you. Now I know ya'll going through a rough time but seeking comfort in someone else ain't gon' solve nothing. If you keep it up, you gon' lose that girl."

"Thanks for the concern Pop but I handled it. I know what I got. I don't wanna lose Meesa but she gotta change too. She got some fucked up ways. She ain't all perfect like she pretends to be."

"We all have demons, son," Ron picked up his glass. "You just gotta find someone whose demons play well with yours."

Gwyn examined herself in the full-length mirror. She thought that she looked great but wondered if her outfit was too much for her date. Cash would be arriving any minute to take her out. He wouldn't tell her where they were going. She hoped that the Balmain fitted, leather jacket, Dolce & Gabbana leather bustier, Alexander Wang army fatigue, high-waisted, pencil skirt and Giuseppe Zanotti Cruel Summer five inch sandals wasn't too much.

All week long she'd thought about backing out but Cash would kill her if she did. She couldn't continue to play him to the left. Either she was going to go all in or leave him the fuck alone. Gwyn was seriously stuck between a rock and a hard place. She genuinely liked him and was honestly starting to care for him. Hell, he was her baby daddy. How could she not feel anything for him?

Cash was unknowingly a big part of her life. She wanted to possibly take things further but allowing herself to love him brought upon too many implications. If she did, she'd eventually have to reveal her secret which could never happen. He'd probably hate her or better yet, wanna locate the child which Gwyn was not down for. Giving her child up for adoption was the best decision for her and the baby's life. Their child was better off with its adoptive parents.

Gwyn didn't want to interrupt the child's life by reentering it. Hell, the child probably didn't even know that it was adopted. There was no need to rock the boat. Secondly, Gwyn had only given her heart to one man to be left broken hearted. After Trey, she swore to never love again. Fuck giving her heart to a man. Loving only brought about heartache.

Gwyn smoothed down her skirt and inhaled deeply. She had a lot to consider but pondering would have to wait. Cash was knocking at her door. Gwyn pulled the door open and greeted him with a warm smile.

"You look beautiful." He took her hand and held her close.

Gwyn felt great in his arms. Her soft breasts pressed against his chest made him want to trace her body with his tongue.

"Thank you." Gwyn stepped back and gave him a once over.

Cash wasn't pulling any punches that night. The man had brought out his Sunday's best. He donned a fitted Tom Ford suit with a white shirt and black skinny tie. On his feet were a pair of fresh out the box Tom Ford oxford shoes. His piercings and tattoos gave the dapper look a thugged out appeal.

"You hot," Gwyn smirked, grabbing her Valentino clutch.

"I try," Cash grinned. "You ready?"

"Yeah. Where are we going though?" She asked locking the door.

"I told you. It's a surprise."

"You and these damn surprise dates ain't gon' worry me."

"Trust me, you'll love it." Cash assured escorting her to his Bugatti.

Cash and Gwyn drove along the highway making small talk while listening to Yo Gotti's trap hit *Sorry*. After a while they arrived at Yankee Stadium. Gwyn was perplexed as to why they were there. It wasn't a game night. Cash parked the car and got out. Gwyn waited as he strolled around the car to open her door. She happily placed her hand in his and stepped out. A brisk wind floated through the air as they made their way through the entrance gate.

"What are we doing here?" She asked.

"You hard headed. I told you it was a surprise."

An eerie quietness swept over the horizon as Gwyn's heels clicked against the cement floor. She'd never been to Yankee Stadium after hours so she didn't know what to expect. As they neared the field, Cash instructed Gwyn to close her eyes. She did as she was asked with baited breath.

"Boy, don't you let me trip and fall," she warned.

"Shut up. I got you." Cash covered her eyes with his hand. "Ok, I need for you to step down."

"What? I don't like this shit at all," Gwyn complained.

"Just step down, girl."

"If I fall that's yo' ass, boy." Gwyn stepped down cautiously.

After bickering back and forth for five minutes, Gwyn finally made it down the flight of steps.

"Ok are you ready?"

"Yes, can I please open my eyes now?"

Cash waited a second and then yelled, "Surprise!"

Gwyn opened her eyes and found R&B crooner Adrian Marcel standing at center field. Beside him was a table set for two. Heaters were placed strategically around the area for warmth. Gwyn couldn't help but smile from ear to ear. She was cheesing so hard her cheeks hurt.

"I can't believe you did all of this for me," she gushed.

"I would do anything for you." Cash placed a soft kiss on her cheek.

Then Adrian parted his lips and started to sing one of Gwyn's favorite songs by him titled *Call You Mine*.

"My darling,
You're the next best thing than air on this earth, baby,
I see you... and somehow you turn my world from dirt to daisies,
I said whatever you want,
Girl, the love we have is written in the sky,
Girl, it's whatever you need,
Tell me all the things you long for and desire."

When Adrian finished singing Gwyn was in tears. The fact that Cash went through the trouble of having her favorite singer come perform for her and setting up a dinner for two at Yankee Stadium was beyond sweet. It was the most thoughtful thing anyone had ever done for her.

"Thank you both for having me. You both have a wonderful night," Adrian
waved goodbye.

"No, thank you!" Gwyn shouted back.

"You like your surprise?" Cash asked.

"Yes." Gwyn hugged him around his neck and kissed him on the lips. "I love it. This is the best surprise I've ever gotten. I am shocked that you went out of your way to do all of this for me. Especially when I have been such a cunt to you," she giggled.

"Yeah, you have been quite a douche." Cash led her over to the table and pulled out her chair.

"You weren't supposed to agree." She side-eyed him.

"I can't front; you were." Cash sat across from her.

"You're right, I was."

"I just wish I knew why." Cash poured her a glass of white wine.

Gwyn's heart rate immediately increased and she felt short of breath. Gwyn stared out into space and tried to steady her breathing.

"You alright?" Cash noticed her skin turning white.

"Huh?" She snapped back to reality.

"The color just left your face. You good? Is it too cold out here for you 'cause we can go inside?"

"No-no, I'm fine." Gwyn situated herself in her seat. "I just had a brain fart."

"Well, I had Chef Éric Ripert prepare us dinner tonight." Cash explained as waiters brought out their meal. "I hope you like seafood."

"I do." Gwyn nodded as the waiters placed before her a plate of wild, striped bass tartare and jicama salad with a champagne mango emulsion.

"This looks delicious."

Gwyn breathed a sigh of relief now that they could concentrate on dinner and not her unwillingness to open up.

"You mind if we say grace?" Cash reached across the table and took her hand.

"Of course not." Gwyn replied caught off guard.

Most men didn't even bother to bless their food before eating. Most men would just go straight to eating. Cash bowed his head.

"Lord, I wanna thank you for bringing Gwyn and I together tonight. God, I thank you for this beautiful woman and this exquisite meal. We ask that this meal nourishes our bodies. In Jesus' name we pray, amen."

"Amen." Gwyn lifted her head. "Thank you for calling me beautiful."

"I'm sure you already know you're fine but it's always nice to hear." Cash took a bite of his fish.

"Yeah, it is, handsome." Gwyn grinned taking a bite as well. "Mmm… this is delicious." She savored the delicious flavors.

"Yeah Chef Ripert did his thing."

"This is amazing." Gwyn gazed around the stadium in awe.

She admired all of the bright lights, green grass, impeccable cleanliness and order. It was as if they were in their own little world. Cash had created their very own oasis inside of the noisy city.

"Thank you for coming out with me tonight," he said sweetly.

"No, thank you for doing all of this. I never, in a million years, would have expected something so extravagant. This must've cost you a fortune."

"A small one but I wouldn't think you would expect anything less," Cash chuckled.

"True." Gwyn giggled.

"Yo," Cash swallowed his food. "Guess what?"

"What?"

"Why I have to fire Dre as my manager?"

"Word?" Gwyn said surprised. "What happened?"

"I found out that nigga was stealing from me. He'd been doing the shit for months."

"Damn, that's fucked up. I'm sorry that happened. You know he's messing with my friend Kelly?"

"Yeah, she better watch herself around that nigga. He ain't no good."

"I'ma tell her." Gwyn said as her cell phone began to ring.

Gwyn reached inside her purse and pulled out her phone. It was Stevie.

"I'm sorry. Let me take this. It's my sister." Gwyn turned to the side and took the call. "Stevie, what is it?"

"Sister!" Stevie cried into the phone.

"What is it? What's wrong?" Gwyn panicked.

"I need you to come get me."

"What happened? Where are you?"

"I'm on the side of the highway."

"What?!" Gwyn shrieked. "What the hell are you doing on the side of the highway?"

"Can you just come and get me, please?" Stevie wailed.

"Yeah, stay on the line. I'm on my way." Gwyn turned to Cash. "Umm… I gotta go."

"What's going on?" Cash asked concerned.

"It's my sister. I have to go pick her up. She's stranded on the side of the highway. I have to get back to my car so I can go get her."

"Naw, I got you. I can take you to go pick her up." Cash stood.

"Thank you." Gwyn got up in a rush.

She and Cash rushed out of the stadium to his car. It seemed like the ride to pick Stevie up took forever. Gwyn held her breath the entire time. It was pitch black and her sister was stranded on the side of the highway. Anything could happen to her as she waited for Gwyn to come to her rescue. She could be hit by a car, kidnapped, anything. Gwyn was deathly afraid for her life.

"Stevie, where are you? We're getting close so flash the flashlight from your phone."

Stevie pressed the flashlight button on her phone and waved her phone in the air.

"There she is!" Gwyn pointed.

Cash quickly pulled over. Gwyn hopped out of the car and rushed over to her sister. There Stevie was on the side of the highway dressed in nothing but a ripped tank top, fitted skirt and Dr. Martens. Her hair was disheveled and she had a few red marks on her face, arms and chest.

"Are you ok?" She asked wrapping Stevie up in her arms.

"Yeah," Stevie nodded her head, holding onto her sister for dear life.

"C'mon and get the car."

Stevie got in the backseat.

"Here, put on my jacket," Gwyn handed it to her.

It was cold and Stevie needed to cover up. Gwyn shut the door and sat back in the passenger seat. Once the coast was clear, Cash pulled back onto the road.

"Now what happened?" Gwyn asked turning around in her seat.

"I was with this guy and we were on our way home from the mall and going out to eat. He decided he wanted to get a room but I wanted to go home because I knew mommy would be home soon from Atlantic City," Stevie sniffled.

"When I told him no he got mad and started going off on me. He started calling me a dick tease and a bitch. He said that he didn't give a fuck what I said, we were gon' smash. I got scared 'cause I thought he was going to rape me, so I told him to pull over and let me out. He wouldn't so I started turning the wheel. When I did, he hit me and we started to bang. When the car started swerving he finally pulled over 'cause he didn't want to get flagged by the police."

"Who is this li'l dude?" Cash asked heated.

"His name is Wiz."

"How old is he?"

"Twenty-seven," Stevie responded reluctantly.

"You've been fuckin' around with a 27 year old?" Gwyn yelled.

"You know where he stay," Cash continued.

"Yeah," Stevie wiped her nose with the back of her hand.

"Ok, you gon' give me his address. I'ma have my people go see about him."

Cash didn't like it when grown men tried to take advantage of little girls.

"I'ma report his ass to the police for messing with an underage girl," Gwyn shot.

"It don't even matter. I won't be seeing him anymore," Stevie mumbled.

"You damn right you won't. What the hell were you thinking Stevie? Oh, my bad. You weren't thinking. That's the problem. You never think 'cause you think yo' ass is grown but as you can see, you're not," Gwyn snapped.

"I knew that something like this was going to happen sooner or later. But no you don't wanna listen to me. Anything could've happened to you tonight. That boy could've raped you, beat you or killed you. You are still just a kid. You walking around here dressing like Nicki Minaj ain't gon' change that. It's only going to put you in grown women situations that yo' li'l ass can't handle."

"I know. I'm sorry," Stevie sobbed.

"No you're not 'cause once this blows over you're going to go right back to acting like a ho!"

"Whoa... Gwyn, chill. You're going too far," Cash intervened.

"I'm sorry," Gwyn fumed. "But talking to her like a decent person doesn't work. There's something wrong wit' her. A year ago she was fine then boom she just changed. What happened? Did somebody touch you? Are you a lesbian and you're afraid to come out? 'Cause if so I don't give a damn about you liking girls. What is it? What is your problem 'cause this shit has to stop?"

"I'M ADOPTED!" Stevie shouted so loud her throat became sore. "I found out that I'm adopted ok!" She wailed like a baby.

Gwyn's heart sank down to her feet. This could not be happening. Not at that moment. Gwyn could feel all of the air from her lungs escape. She felt like she was suffocating. For years she and her mother had done a successful job at keeping the fact that Stevie was adopted a secret. Gwyn had no clue how she could've found out. Maybe she had overheard their mother discussing it with someone. Gwyn just prayed that Stevie hadn't figured out that she was her mother. She always wanted to be the one to tell her daughter the truth.

"What?" Gwyn pretended to be shocked. "That's not true. Who told you that?"

"You ain't gotta front, Gwyn. I know the truth."

Oh my God she knows, Gwyn thought. Lord, help me. What am I going to do? Gwyn glanced over at Cash. She never wanted him to find out this way that he was Stevie's father. She planned on one day revealing the truth but not in this manner. Now was not the time for the truth to be revealed.

"You know the truth about what?" Gwyn played coy.

"I found the adoption papers one day when I was up in the attic going through old baby pics. I had to take a childhood photo to school and I ran across the papers. Mommy adopted me and don't pretend like you didn't know."

Gwyn swallowed hard. She had to tread lightly with her response. She couldn't blow up her spot by saying the wrong thing.

"You're right, I knew. Mommy and I felt it was best you didn't know. We wanted you to have the best life possible," Gwyn replied truthfully.

"We were going to tell you eventually. When we thought you could handle it emotionally."

"Well, you're too late 'cause I already know. It's just messed up 'cause whoever my birth mom is, she didn't even want her name on the adoption papers. The documents said that she wanted her identity to remain unknown. She doesn't want to ever be found, meaning she doesn't love me."

"Ay you don't know that," Cash chimed in. "I'm pretty sure that whoever your birth mom is that she loves you. Putting you up for adoption couldn't have been an easy decision for her."

"It wasn't," Gwyn agreed.

"How do you know?" Stevie eyed her quizzically.

"I mean… I don't know for sure but I can only imagine that the decision was excruciating for her," Gwyn corrected herself. "I'm pretty sure that she was young and scared. I bet if she could take it all back she would."

"I guess," Stevie shrugged as they pulled up to Gwyn and Cash's building.

"C'mon inside. I'ma call mommy and let her know that you're with me."

"You're not going to tell her what happened are you?" Stevie asked on the verge of tears all over again.

"No. We'll keep this just between me and you." Gwyn hugged her daughter.

Their hug lasted for what seemed like eternity.

"Go ahead and go inside. I'll be up in a minute."

"Cash, thank you for bringing my sister to pick me up." Stevie squeezed him tight.

"You good? Anything I can do to help? You get some rest, pretty girl." Cash placed a kiss on the top of her head.

Gwyn's heart soared. The sight of Stevie hugging her father goodnight was priceless.

"Ok." Stevie let go and walked inside the building.

"Well this has been one heck of a night," Cash joked. "Y'all need to go on Maury."

"I am so embarrassed." Gwyn hid her face with her hands.

"Don't be." Cash pulled her hands down and made her look at him. "All families go through stuff. I'm just glad I was here to help."

"Me too. I would've been a wreck without you. One day you're going to make an excellent father." Gwyn envisioned them as a family.

"I'm good," Cash shook his head. "I don't plan on having any kids."

I DON'T GIVE A DAMN
WHAT A HATER SAY.
-CHRISS ZOE FEAT. AV,
"CUT UP"

CHAPTER 17

Meesa, Gwyn and Kelly sat in the office conference room. Meesa was going over ideas for the 2015 fall/winter collection that would show at Mercedes Benz Fashion Week in January. Meesa had to start working on it immediately. Each collection had to be better than the last. As she wrapped up the presentation she couldn't help but notice Kelly's odd behavior. Normally she was the example of professionalism but that afternoon she was out of control.

She kept rubbing her nose and fidgeting around in her seat. One minute she was up out of her seat, then the next she was sitting back down. Meesa would catch her taking selfies and poking at Gwyn like she was a five-year-old. The girl couldn't keep still. For weeks she'd been acting strange. Kelly barely called or hung out with the girls anymore.

She spent all of her spare time with Dre. With him was the only place she wanted to be. But spending so much time with him getting high and having kinky sex was starting to affect her work. Due to her lack of focus, Kelly had mishandled two huge deals with potential buyers. Meesa forgave her because in all of the years they'd worked together Kelly had never mishandled business but the more erratic she behaved, the more she became a concern. Meesa didn't have time to deal with Kelly's erratic behavior though. Her plate was already filled to the brim with her own drama.

"Booooooring! Are we done yet?" Kelly groaned. "'Cause I'm ready to blow this popsicle stand."

"You are on one today." Gwyn laughed surprised by her behavior.

"She sure is." Meesa put the mood boards up. "I'ma slap her rude ass."

"Bye, Fe'Meesa." Kelly burst out laughing.

"What is your problem?"

"I'm happy; is something wrong with that? Is that a crime?" Kelly asked animatedly.

"No, you're just being weird and extra," Meesa frowned.

"Forgive me for living." Kelly waved her off and reached for her purse.

"You know Meesa can't go five minutes without passing judgment on somebody," Gwyn snickered.

"Fuck you!" Meesa flicked her off.

"You gon' be mad but I might have to leave early." Kelly announced looking in her Chanel compact mirror.

"You left early yesterday," Meesa pointed out. "And what's up with the get up?"

Kelly had on a white tank top, skintight jeans and black, thigh high, leather boots.

"Since when you start dressing so sexy?"

"Since I got me some new dick." Kelly popped her lips.

"You changed your hair too because of him?" Meesa asked concerned.

"No, I changed my hair because of me. I wanted to try something different. Do you mind?"

"Speaking of your new dick," Gwyn interjected. "You know Cash fired him, right?"

"No." Kelly replied shocked. "Why?"

"Apparently he caught him stealing money."

"I knew his ass was no good. I ain't never liked him," Meesa confessed.

"When did this happen?" Kelly asked puzzled.

"A few weeks ago," Gwyn replied.

"He never told me that. I was under the impression that he still worked for him."

"Nope, homeboy is on the unemployment line," Gwyn laughed.

"Mmm." Kelly said in disbelief.

She wondered why Dre had kept this information from her. They were together practically everyday. He had ample opportunities to divulge the info. The fact that he would keep such a huge thing under wraps worried Kelly.

"I gotta go pee." She abruptly announced grabbing her purse.

Kelly ran to the restroom and locked herself inside of the handicap stall. She placed the top on the toilet seat down and sat on lid. She had to find out what was going on. Kelly called Dre only for him not to answer. She called him again and got the same results. Panicking, she reached inside her purse and pulled out a small vile of blow.

Kelly swiftly inhaled a few spoonfuls and sat back. *Why isn't he answering,* she thought, calling him again. Dre still didn't answer. The more she called and he didn't pick up caused her to do more and more coke. White residue was all over her nose. Kelly had become addicted to cocaine and she didn't even realize it. Whenever she was angry, paranoid or horny, which seemed to be all of the time now, she did coke.

She'd done a good job at hiding it from everyone but her increasing desire to constantly get high was going to eventually rear its ugly head. Kelly placed a small amount of coke on the tip of her index finger and rubbed it across her gums. This was the feeling she adored. Being high was the best feeling in the world. Kelly felt like she could conquer the world. Picking up her phone, she called Dre's number again. This time he answered.

"Hello? Dre?" Kelly said eagerly into the phone.

"Yeah," he answered groggily.

"Hey, baby, I didn't mean to wake you."

"You good? What's up?"

"Umm, I don't know how to ask you this but did Cash fire you for umm… stealing?"

"Nah, who told you that?" Dre sat up in bed.

"Gwyn. She said that's what Cash told her. She said he fired you a couple weeks ago."

"She got it wrong. I quit 'cause I'm managing Big Sean now," he lied.

"Oh ok," Kelly said relieved. "I'm sorry to call you with that but I just had to know."

"It's cool, but tell yo' homegirl to mind her business," Dre said seriously.

"Shut up," Kelly laughed him off.

"I ain't playing. That bitch need to stay out my fuckin' business," Dre quipped.

"She ain't no bitch," Kelly stuck up for her friend. "I mean, she is sometimes, but she means well. Look, I was just asking you 'cause my friend was concerned."

"I don't give a damn about her being concerned. Like I said, she need to mind her business," Dre shot angrily.

"Calm down baby. I was just asking you a question," Kelly spoke in a soothing tone.

"It's all good," Dre relaxed. "What you doing?"

Kelly looked around and realized that she was sitting in a restroom stall with coke in her lap.

"Ugh, nothing," she lied. "Taking a break."

"You by yourself?"

"Yeah," Kelly smiled wickedly.

"Do me a favor."

"Anything," she swooned.

"Touch yourself."

Kelly happily obliged. She unzipped her jeans and slipped her hand inside. Her finger toyed with her clit until she built up a good rhythm.

"That shit feel good, don't it?" Dre flirted.

"Mmmm hmm," Kelly whimpered in ecstasy.

"You wish I was there with you?"

"Yeeeeessss," she moaned. "Ahhhhhhh! I wish you were here, daddy."

"Come see me. I think somebody's been a bad girl."

Kelly's nipples instantly became aroused.

"I'm cumming!" She shrilled.

"KELLY!" Gwyn called her name, entering the restroom.

Kelly quickly snapped back to reality and stopped stroking her clit. She sat frozen stiff praying to God that Gwyn hadn't heard her.

"I gotta go." She hung up the phone. "Huh?"

"Girl, are you ok? Did you fall in?"

"Nah, here I come."

Kelly put her phone and coke back inside her purse. Using her compact mirror, she made sure that there was no leftover coke residue on her face. There was a little so Kelly wiped it off with her hand. Satisfied with how she looked, she flushed the toilet and stepped out.

"You had to shit or something?" Gwyn eyed her suspiciously. "You've been in here for almost an hour."

"Yeah…" Kelly fibbed washing her hands.

She could barely look at Gwyn. She didn't want her to see the look of dread on her face.

"That breakfast I got from McDonald's must've caught up with me."

"Lies you tell," Gwyn called the bullshit. "Look at me." She made Kelly face her.

Gwyn examined her closely. Kelly's eyes were dilated and she wouldn't stop shaking.

"Let me find out you on some shit we did 10 years ago." Gwyn referred to cocaine.

"Girl, nah," Kelly dismissed the notion. "I'm a mother, chile."

"Remember that." Gwyn warned cryptically.

I KNOW SHE WAS
ATTRACTIVE BUT I
WAS HERE FIRST.
-BEYONCÉ,
"RESENTMENT"

CHAPTER 18

The whole entire house was quiet. Everyone was asleep except for Meesa. She'd put up a brave face for the kids but visions of Black laid up in bed with Brandy haunted her mind. She thought about it day and night. She knew she wasn't crazy. Black had tried to play her out like she was but they'd been down this road before. All of the signs were there.

Knowing now that he was cheating explained his irritable attitude, constant spur-of-the moment trips out of town and emotional detachment. Meesa assumed that her passive aggressive behavior was to blame for their lack luster marriage and sex life but it wasn't. Black apparently had a great sex life. It just wasn't with her. Meesa's stomach turned sour as she sat on the side of the bed.

Tears scorched her cheek. She scrolled through Brandy's Instagram page. There were no pictures of her and Black blatantly out in the open. Meesa had to put on her detective hat and look closer. What she found where pics of Brandy where Black had taken the picture. Meesa could see his reflection in Brandy's glasses. When Brandy took pictures in her car, Black's reflection was on the driver side door.

Meesa wanted to throw up. The more she scrolled, the clearer it became that he'd been cheating on her for months. From the looks of it, seemed like a year. He and Brandy traveled the world together. When she thought he was out of town with his friends or on business, he was really with her. Meesa couldn't stomach looking at another picture.

Her blood was boiling. She could've sworn she stopped breathing. She felt like an absolute idiot. Here she was trying to make their marriage work and this nigga was out cheating. The fact that his mistress was Brandy didn't make it any better. It cut Meesa to the core of her being.

His betrayal was unforgiveable. Nothing could save their marriage now. It was over. She never wanted to see his face again. She didn't even want to breathe the same air he breathed. Meesa got up and rushed to his room. Black was knocked out asleep. He was smiling while he slept. He looked so peaceful. This enraged Meesa. She reached out and grabbed him by his locs. With all of her might, she dragged him out of the bed.

"Who you dreaming about, me or her?" She screamed.

"What?!" Black woke up bewildered.

His body fell to a heap on the floor causing a load thud.

"What the fuck is your problem? You lost you fuckin' mind?" He held the back of his head.

"Get out!" Meesa turned on the light and ran over to his spare closet.

She started to pull his clothes out of the closet one-by-one and throw them at him. Black looked at her like she was insane. Meesa was acting like a madwoman.

"Get yo' lying, cheating as out of my house now!" She hit him in the face with a Timberland boot.

"I ain't going no where!" Black picked up the boot and threw it back at her. "What the fuck is your problem?" He got up from the floor.

"You've been cheating on me with that bitch for a year now!" She threw a stack of pants at him.

"What are you talking about?!" Black dodged the clothes.

"Then you gon' sit there in my face and act like I'm lying! Like I'm fuckin' crazy!" Meesa stopped in disbelief.

"Ain't nobody been cheating on you for a damn year!"

"And you gon' continue to deny it?" Meesa ran up on him. "Lie again! Lie again to my fuckin' face! I dare you!"

"Meesa, you better back yo' ass up," Black shot her a look that could kill.

"What you gon' do, huh? You gon' hit me?"

Black stood still.

"I didn't think so." Meesa mushed him in the forehead.

"Don't touch me no more!" Black shoved her so hard she fell back on the bed.

"Mommy, I can't sleep." Mila came into the room. "You and daddy woke me up."

"Go back to sleep, baby." Meesa shot up from the bed and comforted her.

"Why are you and daddy fighting now?"

"Mommy's allergies are acting up again," Meesa lied.

"Stop lying! Tell her the truth!" Black yelled. "Tell her how you trying to put me out!"

"Ma, why you trying to make pop leave," Kiyan questioned rubbing his eyes.

"You and your sister go back to bed ok." Meesa tried to push them out of the room.

"We can't. Ya'll keep yelling."

"Just do as I say!" Meesa shrieked.

"Don't get mad at us," Mila groaned.

"Say something else, Mila, and I swear to god that's yo' ass!" Meesa warned fed up with her smart mouth.

Kiyan and Mila reluctantly went back to their rooms.

"And Black, I'm not gon' say it again. Get your shit and get out," Meesa's chest heaved up and down. "

"Here you go on that dumb shit you was on ten years ago! Every time we get into it, you wanna put a muthafucka out like this yo' crib!"

"Umm, news flash this is my crib. My name is on the deed. Your criminal ass can't put shit in your name remember?" Meesa shot back.

"You know what man… fuck you!" Black threw up the middle finger at her. "Yo' ass think you better than somebody 'cause you got that lil punk-ass company! Let's not forget who funded that muthafucka. Without me you wouldn't have shit!"

"You wanna throw that bullshit up in my face?" Meesa said appalled. "We can fix that shit right now." She

265

walked out of the room and grabbed her check book and a pen.

"I'll give you your investment back." She came back and stood in his face. "It's not a problem, boo boo. I can write you a check right now. You can cash it as soon as you dot that door!"

"Yo' ass done made a couple of million dollars and lost your fuckin' mind." Black eyed her up and down. "Keep yo' money, Meesa. I don't want it."

"Yeah 'cause all you wanna do is cheat! You ain't nothin' but a cheatin', lying muthafucka. I've been ridin' wit' you for over ten years and this is how you do me?" Her eyes filled with tears.

Meesa eyed Black with contempt. She hadn't felt this weak in years. He'd reduced her to nothing.

"This is how you fuckin' do me after all this time?" She cried like a baby. "What the fuck does this bitch have over me?"

"All you wanna do is bitch and complain," Black countered. "That's not how a marriage works."

"So now everything is my fault?" Meesa scoffed rolling her neck. "You funny. You're real funny. Just get out Black."

"If you keep telling me to get out we don't need to be together." Black began picking up his clothes.

"So you tryna to say you want a divorce?" Meesa made him look at her.

"You said it, I didn't."

"Ok Black now you want a divorce?" Meesa's could feel her heart begin to bleed. "You are so stupid. You go from 0 to 100 real quick but maybe you're right. Maybe we should get a divorce. 'Cause ain't no way in hell, I'ma a stay married to a nigga that can't keep his dick in his pants. You ain't gon' keep cheating on me!"

"If I leave, don't expect me to come back to this muthafucka." Black warned for the last time.

"The door is that way." Meesa pointed.

Black nodded his head. He was beyond heated. If Meesa wanted him gone he was going to give her exactly what she wanted. Black grabbed a shirt and a pair of pants.

"What is going on?" Ron asked from the door.

"I'm getting ready to bounce." Black put on his clothes.

"Son, just calm down. You two need to stop all of this foolishness and talk like two adults," Ron pleaded.

"No, he gots to get the fuck out," Meesa fumed.

"Fuck that," Black placed on his shoes. "She want me to leave then I'm up." He grabbed his car keys. "Tell my kids I love them."

IF YOU WANNA GO
OUT AND BE SINGLE,
GO 'HEAD.
-JASMINE SULLIVAN
FEAT. MEEK MILL,
"DUMB"

CHAPTER 19

Kelly lay in bed asleep. All of the blinds were closed. She didn't want a stitch of sunlight in the bedroom. After her run-in with Gwyn in the ladies restroom, she decided to go cold turkey and quit using coke. It was easier said than done though. After not using for a week, Kelly's entire body crashed. She found herself doing nothing but eating and sleeping. She'd gained five pounds in a week.

She was irritable as hell. Kelly snapped on anyone that came in contact with her. Her friends thought she was either pregnant or on her period. Kelly didn't want to be around anyone so she took a few sick day and stayed at home. She was sound asleep snoring when Jaden woke her up.

"Kelly." He shook her. "Wake up. I got good news."

"Leave me alone," she advised.

"Babe, wake up. I got something I need to tell you." Jaden proceeded to shake her.

"What do you want?" Kelly groaned, turning over onto her back. "Don't you see me trying to sleep?"

"I got good news."

"You're moving out?" Kelly shot sarcastically.

"No." Jaden ignored her sarcasm.

"Then it ain't good news then." Kelly laughed at herself.

"Whatever, man. Guess what? I got a gig." Jaden exclaimed excited.

"Good for you. Now can I go back to sleep?" Kelly huffed, turning back over onto her stomach.

"I got hired at General Motors. You ain't happy for me?"

"No, I'm not. You don't get no damn brownie points for getting a damn job," Kelly scowled.

"What's wrong wit' you? You ain't been nothing but a bitch here lately. What you got you a nigga or something?" Jaden shot.

"Yep, I sure do," Kelly shot. "And he's ten times the man you'll ever be so get the fuck outta my face. You and yo' li'l wack-ass GM job can both kiss my ass. Now get out!" Kelly snatched the covers and placed them over her head.

Jaden was stunned at her reaction. He thought she'd be happy that he'd finally found work. He kind of figured that she'd found a little friend. Kelly was hardly ever home. The smell of another's man's cologne on her clothes said it all. But never did he think she'd be bold enough to admit it. Jaden thought that maybe their relationship could be salvaged but after Kelly's rant, he was done fucking with her for good.

"Man, fuck you!" He snatched the covers from off of her. "I don't know who the fuck you think you talkin' to. Don't let that new dick you suckin' get you fucked up!"

"Jaden, you better go on. I ain't in the fuckin' mood!" Kelly tried pulling the covers back to no avail.

"You ain't in the mood to do shit lately. You ain't in the mood to be around yo' son, to go to work', nothin! Look at you." He glared at her with pure disgust in his eyes. "You look a mess. You look like a fuckin' crackhead. What he do; stop fuckin' wit' you? You took off work 'cause you in yo' feelings?"

"You wish," Kelly rolled her eyes knowing he was telling the truth.

Kelly was a wreck. She'd lost ten pounds and begun to form dark circles under her eyes.

"You wish he'd stop fuckin' wit' me, don't you; so I can come running back to you?"

"Nah, I wish you would start acting like the old Kelly and get your shit together! If not for yourself, then for your fuckin' son!" Jaden threw the covers in her face and stormed out of the room.

The girls didn't venture out to Brooklyn too often but when they did, they always made it their business to visit Body by Brooklyn Day Spa. Body by Brooklyn was a 10,000 square feet luxury complex with 10 treatment rooms and a V.I.P suite. The facility offered massages, facials, lash extensions, Botox and waxing. With all of the drama Meesa had going on in her life, she was well over due for a waxing. All of the girls were there except for Kelly who had been M.I.A lately. Meesa and the girls sat in the private V.I.P suite draped in fluffy, white robes and slippers.

"Would you ladies like a glass of wine or champagne?" One of the attendants asked.

Everyone said yes except for Meesa.

"I need something stronger than wine or champagne. I need a double shot of something, so no wine for me."

Nikki, Gwyn and Destiny did a double take. Meesa never drank alcohol.

"Ok, the sky must be falling if yo' ass talking about drinking." Destiny spoke stunned. "What's going?"

"Giiiiiiirl… my life has been turned upside down." Meesa tried her best to hold back the tears that were dying to escape.

"What's wrong, friend?" Nikki scooted closer and wrapped her arm around her.

"That was Black on that picture."

"I knew it!" Gwyn slapped her hand against her knee. "I called that shit," she gloated.

"Are you done?" Meesa scowled.

"Oh, I'm sorry," Gwyn straightened up.

"Damn, I thought everything was good between ya'll?" Destiny said puzzled.

"Me too," Nikki co-signed.

"I ain't wanna tell ya'll but we've been having problems for the last two years. I guess he got fed up and started cheating this year."

"Why you ain't tell us?" Destiny asked.

"I was embarrassed. Everybody thinks that we have this perfect relationship—"

"No, that's what you want everybody to think," Gwyn interjected. "I knew better. Ain't no relationship peaches and cream all the damn time. Everybody go through shit, even Jay-Z and Beyoncé. Solangegate proved that."

"Here you are, ladies." The attendant handed them their drinks.

"Thank you." The ladies said in unison.

"So what happened when you confronted him?" Nikki questioned.

"He denied it of course," Meesa rolled her eyes. "I knew he would. Black just ain't gon' come out and admit it."

"Mmm-mmm-mmm-mmm," Gwyn pursed her lips and shook her head. *"These niggas ain't loyal,"* she sang.

"You got that right," Meesa complied. "That's why I put his ass out."

"Girl, you put Black out?"

"I sure in the hell did. He wanna stick his dick in another woman then he needed to get the fuck out. Plain and simple. I ain't gon' sit up there and put up with that shit. I told him before we got married that if ever cheated on me again that it was a wrap and I meant it."

"So you gon' file for divorce?" Nikki asked visibly sadden by the news.

"I mean, I guess I have no choice," Meesa shrugged her shoulders.

"What does he see in her cause she is ghetto as hell." Destiny shot a look of pure disgust.

"That's probably what he like. She's still the same hoodrat bitch she was ten years ago and I'm not. Black like all that ole ratchet-ass shit."

"Well if you wanna keep yo' husband, you better get to liking ratchet shit too," Gwyn quipped.

"I think not." Meesa spat offended. "If he can't accept me the way I am then fuck him."

"Girl bye. You don't mean that." Gwyn waved her off. "You better get it together, bitch. You have let all of this glitz and glamour go to yo' head. You are still the same ghetto Meesa that use to sit on my mama porch and eat Miracle Whip sandwiches with me."

Meesa couldn't help but crack up laughing at the memory.

"It's ok to elevate your life but you can't ever forget where you come from. You married a thug. Er' now and then you gotta get on some gangsta shit with that nigga.

Balance it all out. 'Cause guess what? What you won't do, another bitch surely will," Gwyn advised.

Meesa rolled her eyes and groaned. Her friend was right. If she looked closely she would see that Black wasn't all to blame for their troubles. She'd played a part in it too. She never supported anything Black wanted to do. It was always her way or the highway. Maybe she could loosen up some but that didn't take away the fact that her husband had cheated on her. Some things just couldn't be tolerate or forgiven.

I CAN'T LIVE A LIE.
-MILEY CYRUS,
"WRECKING BALL"

CHAPTER 20

Flickers of light from the fire place danced across Gwyn's naked body as she lay snuggled up in Cash's arms. They'd been making love for hours. She couldn't get enough of him. Cash did things with his tongue that should be illegal in all 50 states. He knew exactly how to take her body to the brink of convulsions.

For the past week she'd been trying to figure out a way to tell him about Stevie but the words never seemed to come out right. Cash not wanting children put a monkey wrench in everything. There was no way she was going to tell him about Stevie, then he turn around and shun her. Maybe it was a good thing that he didn't know. Gwyn still had time to back out. She could cut things off with Cash, move out of the building and never see him again.

"You know I think I'm starting to fall in love with you." Cash whispered into her ear.

"You don't mean that." Gwyn lay frozen stiff.

"Why would I lie? I don't lie about my feelings."

"Cash..." Gwyn searched her mind for the right words to say.

"What?" He kissed her on the forehead.

"Don't you think we're moving too fast?"

"Nah, I know how I feel. The question is do you feel the same?" He looked down at her.

Gwyn could lie there and pretend like she didn't love Cash but that would just be a lie. She was over the moon for him. He didn't back down when she tried to run and hide. He stood firm in his feelings for her. He made her feel safe and secure. She knew that when times got rough his love for her wouldn't waiver.

"I love you too," she admitted.

"I know you do. How could you not love me? I'm sexy as hell," he joked.

"Shut up." Gwyn playfully hit him on the chest.

"You love me enough to go get me some Chipotle? I'm starving."

"Look at you." Gwyn sat up. "Yeah, I'll go but don't make this a habit."

After showering Gwyn was dressed and out the door. Cash took a shower after her. D'Angelo bumped through the surround sound speakers as he placed on lotion. Cash was so into the music that he didn't even hear the doorbell ring. Stevie rang the bell several times before using her key. She heard music playing so she knew her sister was at home.

Stevie had caught the train all the way into the city so she could get her sister's help. She was so upset with their mother that she couldn't think straight. She needed Gwyn's advice on how to confront their mother about the adoption. She couldn't do it by herself. She needed her sister's support.

"Sister!" Stevie called out, taking off her jacket.

Not getting a response, she gravitated towards Gwyn's bedroom where the music was coming from.

"Sister!" She called out again entering the room.

"Oh shit!" Cash shouted covering up his private parts with his hand.

"Oh my God. I'm sorry." Stevie spun around covering up her eyes.

She'd seen Cash's full package and was pleased with the result. His body reminded her of a Greek god. Cash quickly slipped on a pair of hooping shorts and a tee-shirt.

"You can turn around now." He said turning down the volume on the music.

"I am so sorry. I had no idea you were here," Stevie blushed.

"You good. Your sister didn't tell me you were coming by," Cash responded still flustered.

Stevie wore a Dymes sports bra and jogging pants. Her breasts were way too big for the small top.

"She didn't know I was coming." Stevie eyed him lustfully.

Cash was fine as fuck and she wanted a piece of him.

"Where is my sister anyway?" Stevie posed sexily.

"She ran out to go get us something to eat." Cash replied feeling uncomfortable. "How about we go in the living room?" He tried to walk past her.

"Hold up." She reached out and grabbed his hand. "Now that I have you here. I wanna tell you thank you again for the other night. No man has ever been there for me like that."

"You're welcome." Cash tried to pull his hand away but Stevie held on tight.

"No, it really meant a lot to me. I see why my sister is so into you."

"I'm into her too," Cash yanked away.

"What you doing? Stop. I just wanna repay you."
Stevie stood on her tippy toes and kissed him.

"Stevie, what the fuck are you doing?!" Gwyn
screamed at the top of her lungs.

Neither Cash nor Stevie had heard her come in.

"Nothing!" Stevie jumped back. "I was just telling
him thank you for the other night."

"No the fuck you weren't! You were kissing him!"
Gwyn's lips trembled as she pushed her down onto the
ground. "Do you know what you've done? Do you know
what you did?" She hit Stevie repeatedly on the arm.

"I'm sorry! It was just an innocent kiss!" Stevie
tried blocking her hits.

"Gwyn, chill!" Cash pulled her off of her. "She's
just a child! She doesn't know what she's doing!" Cash
tried to reason with Gwyn who was freaking out.

"No, it's not ok!" Gwyn jerked crying
uncontrollably. "It's not ok! She's your fuckin' daughter!"

"What?" Cash screwed up his face, confused.

"I didn't know how to tell you but when we hooked
up that night in Atlanta, I got pregnant!"

"What?" Cash took a step back.

"I got pregnant and I was scared and I didn't know
what to do so I gave the baby up for adoption. I gave my

baby girl to my mother. Stevie is my daughter! She's our daughter," Gwyn cried.

The room fell silent. The only sound that was heard was the sound of Gwyn sobbing.

"You stupid bitch!" Stevie snapped getting up from the floor. "How could you do this to me? You knew you were my mother this whole time and you didn't say a thing?" Tears fell from her eyes.

"I'm sorry."

"Fuck you." Stevie pushed by her and ran out of the house.

Cash stood silent. He couldn't comprehend the news that was given to him. He was stunned to say the least. He didn't know what was real and what was fake. He'd just told the woman standing before him that he loved her. Now she was telling him that they had a 14-year-old daughter together that he thought was her sister.

"Say something," Gwyn cried.

Cash didn't have anything to say. He had to go. He had to get out of there. He didn't utter a word. He walked right past Gwyn as if she didn't exist.

"Cash, wait! Let me explain!"

Cash ignored her cries and continued to walk away. He didn't give a fuck about her tears. He had to get out of there before he killed her.

A full month had gone by since Meesa put Black out. He'd been staying at the Trump SoHo hotel ever since. Living in a hotel on a full-time basis wasn't an ideal situation for Black. He hated it. He missed his kids terribly. He wasn't used to being away from them for so long. He was used to waking up to them running around the house like two wild banshees. He missed their laughter and how their eyes lit up whenever he walked through the door.

Seeing them only on the weekends was killing him softly. But this was the consequence he had to pay for being unfaithful. He and Meesa weren't even speaking terms. He didn't have anything to say her and vice versa.

The two of them were in a bitter standoff with one another. Neither was willing to give in or be the first apologize. Black knew he should've said he was sorry but his pride had gotten in the way. Meesa had put him out of his own house and made him look like a monster in front of their kids. Black didn't have shit to say to her. He'd apologize to her when he felt like it.

It was the weekend. Black entered Kiyan's school gymnasium to pick him up from basketball practice. Kiyan walked towards him dressed in his white and green basketball uniform. A big duffle bag swung from his shoulder. Kiyan's body was filled with sweat and he had an angry expression on his face.

"What's up, man?" Black tried to high-five him.

"Hey," Kiyan spoke.

He didn't even bother to raise his hand to high-five his dad. He wasn't in the mood to be playful.

"What's wrong wit' you?" Black asked concerned.

"Nothing." Kiyan walked right past him.

"Whoa, hold up. Where you going?" Black pulled him back.

"To the car. We gotta go pick up Mila from ballet class, don't we?" Kiyan said with an attitude.

"Nah, we ain't going no where until you tell me what your problem is." Black sat down on one of the bleachers. "I got all day."

Kiyan dropped his duffle bag on the floor and watched as his teammates filed out of the gymnasium.

"Talk to me," Black said.

"Are you and ma getting a divorce 'cause all of my friends say if ya'll do that I'll hardly ever see you again? Then what's gonna happen to us?"

Black sat speechless. He normally had an answer for Kiyan's questions but this time he had no clue as to how to reply. He didn't know where he and Meesa stood. Divorce could very well be on the horizon. Yet again, neither of them had pulled the trigger so maybe there was still hope for them after all.

"Come here, man." Black pulled his son close and made him sit next to him. "I know me and yo' mom being separated is tough. I never meant for anything of this to happen but what's going on between me and her has nothing to do with you."

"See, that's were you're wrong. It has everything to do with me. You're not the one who hears Mila crying herself to sleep every night. I do. You're not the one who hears ma playing sad music when we go to bed. I do. Hell, she don't even wanna get up and cook half of the time now."

"She's really been sad?" Black said astonished.

"Yeah, you let her down. You let us down."

Black's heart broke in a million pieces. He always swore that he would be a better father to his kids than his father was to him. Now here he was disappointing them. He remembered feeling anger and sorrow when his father would yell and hit his mother. His kids had witness him and Meesa go at it one too many times.

That wasn't the example he wanted to set for them. He wanted his kids to be proud of him. He wanted his family back. Cheating and arguing wasn't the way to communicate his frustrations with Meesa. If he did nothing else, he had to attempt to at least talk to her once.

YOU TOOK MY HEART
AND REARRANGED IT
AND NOW YOU HAVE
FULL CONTROL.
-TREY SONGZ, "FIND A
PLACE"

CHAPTER 21

"What if she's dead?" Destiny said as she and the girls got off the elevator on Gwyn's floor.

"Shut up! Don't say that," Nikki hissed pushing her in the arm.

"Well, what if?" Destiny shrugged. "According to y'all the bitch ain't been to work in two weeks.

"She hasn't but I don't think she's dead," Meesa responded. "At least I hope not," she said placing her key in the door.

She and the girls stepped inside of Gwyn's apartment to find it was a mess. Gwyn's place was normally immaculate but there were pizza boxes, Chinese takeout, clothes and tissue thrown everywhere. There was even a foul stench in the air. It smelled like feet and musty balls.

"Ugh, I'ma throw up," Destiny covered her nose.

"Shit, me too," Meesa agreed stepping around carefully.

She didn't want to get anything on her brand new Louboutin's.

"Me three." Nikki almost threw up for real.

"What in the hell is going on?" Meesa said disgusted as Ferragamo begun to bark. "Gwyn!"

"Huh?" Gwyn mumbled, crying.

"Where are you?" Meesa looked around.

"I'm over here," she whimpered.

Meesa followed the sound of her voice and found her sitting on the kitchen floor eating a bowl of ice cream and pickles. Tears streamed down her face.

"Girl, what the hell are you doing?" Meesa turned on the kitchen light.

"Suffering."

"We see that. It look like the Walking Dead up in here." Destiny looked around praying a bug wouldn't crawl on her.

"What happened?" Meesa sat on the floor next to Gwyn.

"Stevie won't talk to me."

"What's new?" Meesa spat sarcastically.

"Neither will Cash," Gwyn sobbed.

"Why not?"

"Yo' mama needs to give Stevie bad ass a whooping," Destiny popped her lips.

"That's the problem. It's my fault that she acts the way she does," Gwyn hung her head low.

"How is it your fault? Your mama is the one not steppin' up to the plate," Meesa disagreed.

"You don't get it. Stevie is adopted."

"Giiiiiiirl, the devil is a liar!" Destiny waved her hands in the air like an old woman in church.

"Stevie is adopted?" Nikki gasped.

"Yeah, my mother adopted her because she is my daughter."

"You say what now?" Meesa leaned forward so she could hear better.

"Back in '99 when I was living in Atlanta, I met Cash. We hooked up and I got pregnant. I wasn't ready to be a mom so I gave my baby up for adoption. My mother adopted the baby. I never thought I'd see Cash again. Hell, I didn't even know his name. Then I come home the other day and I see Stevie kissing her father. I freaked out and told both of them everything. They haven't spoken to me since." Gwyn wailed like a baby.

"I don't know what I'm going to do."

"I can't believe you held this from us all these years," Meesa said stunned.

"I couldn't risk the truth ever coming out."

"Girl, I can't," Destiny shook her head. "Y'all bitches and y'all chamber of secrets ain't gon' bother me."

"I wish you would've felt comfortable enough with us to tell us. We wouldn't have judged you," Nikki reasoned.

"I know," Gwyn sniffed. "I was just ashamed. I don't know what I'ma do y'all. I gotta get them to talk to me. I've called, texted and emailed but ain't neither one of them fuckin' with me."

"Stop calling and go see them face-to-face," Meesa advised.

"I'm scared though. What if they cuss me out?"

"You gon' have to sit there and take it. What you did was fucked up, so you have to accept whatever they give you."

"You're right," Gwyn nodded her head. "That's what I'ma do. I'ma go see them."

Gwyn mustered up the courage of mustard seed and went to the studio to visit Cash. She'd found out through social media that he was there. She knew he wouldn't be happy to see her but she had to talk to him. They had to lay everything out on the table. Now that he knew he was Stevie's father, she had to know if he wanted to be a part of her life. Their daughter desperately needed them both.

Gwyn was prepared for him to tell her to leave and to never come back. She couldn't be mad if he never wanted to see her face again. She didn't deserve his sympathy or kindness. She hadn't earned it. Gwyn hadn't been upfront with him. She'd kept life-changing information from him. If she received a negative reaction from him, then that was exactly what she deserved.

Gwyn's hand trembled as she checked her face in the rearview mirror. She looked as good as she was going to look. She rocked a super laid back look. She wore pale pink lip gloss with a cat eye. On her body she wore a black, Pretty Ratchet Things sweatshirt, graphic print, black and white leggings and J's. Her hair was pulled up in a sloppy bun. A small set of diamond stud earrings shined from her ears.

Gwyn grabbed her Balenciaga bag and got out of the car. She fearfully walked inside. Cash was in studio D.

Gwyn inhaled deep and opened the door. A cloud of weed smoke hit her smack dab in the face as soon as she walked in. Once her eyes adjusted to the smoke and dimly lit lights, she found Cash sitting at the mixing board. Cash noticed her out of the corner of his eye and said, "What are you doing here?"

"Hi," Gwyn spoke softly.

"What you doing here?" He ice grilled her.

"I came to talk to you. Can I sit down?" Gwyn pulled out a chair.

"Just say what you gotta say so I can get back to work," Cash said, clearly annoyed by her presence.

"First off, I want to say that I'm so sorry, Cash, for keeping Stevie a secret. I should've told you that day at lunch when we first went out but I was just too afraid. Then you said that you didn't want any kids so that really fucked me up. I didn't think that I would ever be able to tell you the truth. It should've never got this far. I know it's all my fault. You and Stevie deserved better from me and I let the both of you down."

"My fuckin' daughter kissed me, man. You know how fucked up that is?" Cash questioned about to flip.

"I know." Gwyn began to cry. "I wish that shit wouldn't have ever happened."

"Tell me about it." Cash leaned back in his seat.

"I really wanna make things right. I wanna step up to the plate and be a mother to Stevie. She deserves to have her real mother take care of her."

"She does," Cash agreed.

"I need your help though. I mean, I can do this by myself but I would much rather have you by my side," Gwyn reasoned.

Cash stared off into space. He'd never envisioned himself as a father. He never planned on having children but now that he knew Stevie was his, he felt inclined to be there for her. She needed a strong male figure in her life. Cash honestly couldn't wait to make up for all the time they'd lost.

"I'm down." He finally said.

"Really? You really wanna help me with Stevie?" Gwyn said optimistically.

"Yeah."

"Oh thank God." Gwyn jumped up and hugged him around his neck.

"Uh ah, bruh, we ain't there yet." He gently pushed her back.

"Sorry." Gwyn regained her composure.

"Will you go with me to pick her up from school? Stevie hasn't answered any of my calls since she left that day."

"Yeah."

Gwyn and Cash left the studio and headed over to Stevie's school. When they got there they quickly learned that Stevie hadn't been to school that whole entire week. The school was threatening to expel her. Gwyn didn't know whether to scream or cry. Stevie was on a path of destruction. Gwyn and Cash quickly left the school and went to her mother's house. Regina stood at the door awaiting their arrival.

"Hi, mama." Gwyn kissed her on the cheek. "Is Stevie home yet?"

"No. I don't know where she is. She's not answering any of my calls either," Regina replied.

"This child is determined to give me a heart attack." Gwyn sat down on the couch.

Cash sat beside her.

"So you're the baby daddy?" Regina sat opposite of them.

"It seems so." Cash responded still soaking the information in.

"As you can see, you and Gwyn have a lot on your hands. Now that Stevie knows the truth, it's time you two take over and start raising her yourself. I'm still going to be here to help but my raising babies days are done. Gwyn, it's time for you to be the mother she so desperately needs. 'Cause I can't do it no more. I'm old. Shit, I'm tired."

"That's what I plan on doing," Gwyn responded. "The first fourteen years of her life I failed her. I wanna rectify that."

"Give me her number," Cash said. "I'ma try calling her from my phone. She might answer 'cause she doesn't know my number."

Gwyn gave Cash Stevie's number as he requested. He let the phone ring until her voicemail picked up then he hung up.

"Oh my God," Gwyn shrilled, placing her face into her hands. "Why won't this child answer the phone?"

"I just hope she's ok." Cash said genuinely worried.

"We just have to sit and wait for her to come home. She has to come home eventually."

For the next several hours Gwyn and Cash sat frantically awaiting Stevie's arrival. They continued to try to call her phone to no avail. Every time a car passed by, Gwyn would hop up and look out the window to see if it was her only to be disappointed when it wasn't. It didn't help that she felt nauseated. For the past month Gwyn had been having spouts of feeling queasy and constantly tired.

She didn't know if it was because of all the stress she was under lately or if she was pregnant. She was honestly too afraid to find out. Cash had just accepted the fact that he had one child. He would probably lose it if he learned he possibly had another one on the way.

By nightfall Gwyn was a wreck. Stevie normally would've at least checked in with someone by now but she hadn't. Gwyn prayed that she hadn't pushed her to the brink of running away. She wouldn't be able to handle it. As she sat resting her head on Cash's shoulder, the sound of the front door opening alarmed her. Stevie was home. Gwyn didn't even let her get good through the door before she bombarded her with a ton of questions.

"Where have you been? Why haven't you been answering your phone? We've been trying to call you all day. Don't you know we've been worried sick about you?" Gwyn yelled pulling her into her embrace.

"Get off of me!" Stevie pushed her away. "Don't pull that mother of the year bullshit on me. Let's not forget, I know you," Stevie snapped.

"Now, if you'll excuse me, I'm going up to my room." Stevie attempted to walk up the steps.

"No you're not." Gwyn pulled her back down. "You're coming home with me."

"Girl, bye. No I'm not. I'm not going nowhere with you or him." Stevie pointed to Cash whom she could barely look at in the eye.

She was beyond embarrassed. She'd thrown herself at her father. Stevie never wanted to see Cash or Gwyn's faces again for as long as she lived.

"I know this situation is fucked up and it is all my fault but I'm gonna make it right." Gwyn pleaded with tears in her eyes.

"On everything I love, I'm gonna do right by you, Stevie. You didn't deserve any of this and if it takes the rest of my life, I'm gonna make it up to you. I just need you to give me a chance to fix this."

"We both," Cash stood up. "…wanna fix this. It's weird as fuck, considering everything that has happened but we can get through this… as a family."

Stevie looked at Gwyn and Cash. For the past year she'd wondered and daydreamed about her birth parents. She wondered how they looked, how they smiled and how they laughed. She wondered if she resembled them. She wondered if they thought about her or missed her. She wondered did they regret their decision.

Because of Gwyn's selfish choice, for the past year Stevie had felt thrown away and unloved. She searched for acceptance and love from every man she met. The only way she knew how to get it was by being sexual. No one paid attention to her before she started acting out. Gwyn was too busy living her life in the city and Regina was too old and tired to give her the appropriate attention she craved.

Stevie figured negative attention was better than none. Once she found the adoption papers that was her excuse to let loose. She was pissed and angry at the world. She didn't know who she was anymore. Now she stood face-to-face with the two people who had given her life. She didn't know how to feel about either of them. She hated her sister/mother for lying to her.

She barely knew Cash. He seemed to be a great guy but how could she ever face him knowing she'd kissed him in the mouth? Hell, just a few weeks before she had a major crush on him. The mere thought of it made Stevie want to throw up.

The fact still remained that Cash and Gwyn were her parents. No matter if she liked it or not, she was stuck with them. They were going to be in her life forever. Stevie didn't want to live with Gwyn but she knew she didn't have any choice. She'd give it a month and if she hated it, Stevie was going to pack her bags and run away for good.

AS MUCH AS I WANT
TO DENY, I HATE OUR
FAIRYTALE HAD TO
END.
-SYLEENA JOHNSON
"PERFECTLY
WORTHLESS"

CHAPTER 22

Alex Isley played softly while Meesa stood over the hot stove preparing dinner. Black would be arriving shorty so they could sit down and talk. She was making his favorite meal: fried chicken, corn, mash potatoes and gravy. Meesa wasn't looking forward to the sit down 'cause she figured they'd be doing nothing but arguing. If they did start fighting, she had something up her sleeve to calm Black right on down.

Thankfully, the kids wouldn't have to sit through another grudge match. They were gone to the movies with their grandpa. Meesa battered a piece of chicken and sang along to Alex Isley's song *Still Care*. The words mimicked her life.

> *"Broken retrospective*
> *A part of love still lives*
> *Trying to forget when there's so much to forgive.*
> *After all this time*
> *Can't believe that I, still care."*

Meesa closed her eyes for a second and let the music soak in. She was a nervous wreck. Every time she heard the elevator doors open her palms began to sweat. Life without Black hadn't been the easiest but it had been the best decision for both of them. They needed the time apart to reevaluate themselves and their marriage. She didn't know what their conversation would bring but she hoped they would each leave with some type of resolution and clarity.

Black got off the elevator. He felt like he was on foreign territory. He hadn't been home since the day he left. Black pulled out his house keys and attempted to unlock the door. He quickly realized that his key no longer worked. Meesa had changed the locks.

"This chick here." He groaned knocking on the door.

Meesa jumped. The sound of Black knocking startled her. Swallowing hard, she turned the fire off on the stove and opened the door.

"Hey." She spoke holding the door open.

"What's up?" Black crossed the threshold and entered his home.

Everything was the same as he left it.

"What made you change the locks? I told you I wasn't coming back to this muthafucka." He quipped taking off his jacket.

"You're here now aren't you? Besides, I wanted to make sure I didn't have any unwelcomed guests." Meesa shot back.

"Ah huh," Black chuckled. "It's smelling good up in here. What you cook?"

"All of your favorites." Meesa skipped into the kitchen.

"Oh word? That was nice. What made you do that?"

"I just figured I'd something nice since this may be our last meal together." Meesa placed the food on the table family style.

"You ain't put nothing in it did you?" Black eyed her skeptically.

"Of course not." Meesa replied sweetly taking her seat.

She and Black both bowed their heads and said grace.

"Amen," Black said going straight for the mash potatoes and gravy.

It was his favorite.

"I wasn't expecting you to cook so shout out to you for that."

"Mmm hmm it's all good." Meesa fixed her plate. "So what do you wanna talk about?"

"We need to figure this shit, out man. I mean, I know I fucked up. I shouldn't have done what I did. That shit wasn't cool."

"And what exactly did you do?" Meesa pierced her eyes at him.

Black had yet to admit that he'd cheated on her.

"You know what I did, man. You don't know need to hear me say it."

"If you can't even say it out loud, then there ain't no point in us even talking." Meesa began to eat everything on her plate besides the mash potatoes and gravy.

Black filled his chest with air and sighed heavily.

"Ok, I cheated on you with Brandy. Is that you wanna hear? Does that make you feel better?" He took a bite of his chicken.

"No, it doesn't make me feel better. At least you manning up and telling me the truth instead of lying to me. You was straight trying to play me like I was crazy."

"Yeah, I know. That wasn't cool." Black devoured his mash potatoes.

"No it wasn't." Meesa gulped down her glass of wine. "It was foul as hell."

Meesa felt herself getting upset. She swiftly grabbed the bottle of wine and poured herself another drink. Black took the spoon for the mash potatoes and refilled his plate.

"What you put in these mash potatoes? These muthafucka's are fire." He lathered on a ladle full of gravy.

"Nothing; just the usual." Meesa eyed him devilishly. "Just tell me. What made you do it and why did you do it with Brandy of all people?"

"To be honest wit' you." Black swallowed a mouth full of mash potatoes. "It was just something that happened. It wasn't something that I was looking for. I seen her out in Vegas one night and we just ended up kicking it. It was just nice to be around somebody who wasn't always talking about work or belittling me for the shit I like to do."

"That's some bullshit." Meesa leaned back in her seat heated.

"What; you wanted to know the truth so I'm giving it to you." Black placed down his fork. "You never wanna do anything with me. Hell, the only time you wanna give me some pussy is when you mad at me. You wanna drag me to all of these swanky-ass parties but whenever I ask you to do one thing for me, you get to talking a bunch of shit."

"No, I don't," Meesa challenged.

"So I'm lying?" Black cocked his head to the side.

"No, you're not lying," she huffed. "I know that things between us haven't been perfect but that still doesn't give you the right to go out and cheat and with Brandy no less. You know how bad that shit hurt me? You know how I feel about that bitch. Do you have feelings for her? Do you love her?"

"Nah, I don't love her. She was just cool to kick it wit' that's all. Brandy just let me be. She doesn't try to change me and sometimes I feel that's what you want. I feel like you want me to be somebody that I'm not."

"Black, I love you. I just don't like some of the decisions that you make. I understand you helping Victor out but at some point you gon' have to let all this street shit go. I don't want my kids around that stuff."

"I understand," Black paused.

His stomach had begun to hurt.

"Mmm… I think I might've eaten too fast."

"Maybe." Meesa drank her wine.

"You barely touched your food." He noticed.

"I didn't have much of an appetite."

"So what you wanna do, man?" Black massaged his stomach.

"I wanna slap the shit outta you. I wanna spit in your face, that's what I wanna do," Meesa spat.

"We both know that ain't gon' happen."

"Don't be so sure," she fired back.

"Man fuck!" Black's stomach churned. "What the fuck man?" He hunched over and laid his head on the table.

Sweat beads poured from his forehead.

"It hurt don't it?" Meesa questioned.

"Huh?" Black looked up in agony.

"Your stomach… It hurts doesn't it?"

"Yeah," Black winced.

"Now maybe you can understand what the last month has felt like for me."

"What the fuck did you do?" Black yelled feeling a load of shit drop down to his anus.

"I put a little something in the mash potatoes and gravy that you love so much."

"What you put in my food?" Black shot up from his seat.

"Calm down. It's just a few laxatives," Meesa chuckled polishing off the rest of her wine.

"I could kick yo' ass!"

"Not if you don't shit on yourself first." She died laughing.

"Man, I swear to god I'ma fuck you up!" Black ran to the bathroom.

Meesa followed behind him. She had to hold her stomach she was laughing so hard.

Black held on to the back of his ass and tried to turn the knob on the bathroom door but found it locked.

"What the fuck is the bathroom door doing locked!" He shrilled.

"Oh it is? Damn," Meesa grinned.

"I'ma fuckin' kill you!" Black ran to their master bathroom but found that door locked too.

"MEESA, UNLOCK THE FUCKIN' DOOR! I'MA SHIT ON MYSELF!" Black squeezed his ass checks together tight.

"I don't know where the key is." She played coy.

"MEESA, BABY PLEASE! I BEG YOU! OPEN THE FUCKIN' DOOR!" Black tried his best to hold it together.

Meesa could see that he was seconds away from crapping his self so she pulled the key out of her bra and unlocked the door.

Black sprinted into the bathroom and slammed the door behind him.

"You make it to the toilet, baby?" Meesa laughed hysterically.

"That shit ain't funny!" Black yelled sitting down on the toilet.

"Oh, yes it is. It's fuckin' hilarious." Meesa sat on the floor outside the door.

"So this is your way of getting back at me?" Black groaned.

"A little bit. You will never know how bad this shit hurts," Meesa replied seriously as tears came to her eyes.

"I'm sorry," Black replied sincerely.

"I know you are. I just don't know if this time I'm sorry is good enough."

MY FOOLISH HEART
WILL TRUST JUST
ANYONE, IT'S SO
NAÏVE.
-JASMINE SULLIVAN,
"MY FOOLISH HEART"

CHAPTER 23

Whenever Kelly wasn't tied up at Dre's place or at work she'd meet up with him for coffee. That particular morning, Dre stood outside of Starbucks awaiting her arrival with two cups of Joe in hand. The cold brisk wind pierced his skin. Kelly greeted him with a huge smile. Seeing his face always made her happy. Now that she'd lain off coke, he was her only drug of choice.

"Morning, daddy." She kissed his cheek.

"Morning." He handed her the cup of coffee.

"How are you this morning?"

"Great now that I'm with you," Kelly beamed.

"Let's take a walk."

"Ok." Kelly took a sip from the cup.

The hot coffee slid down her throat with velvet ease.

"Have you been having fun with me these last few months?" Dre quizzed.

"Yes, of course. Meeting you is one of the best things that has ever happened to me."

"I feel the same way." He wrapped her up in his arms. "You're a really cool girl, Kelly, and the turn up with you has been real. I never knew you were as wild as you are. When that red dot come on, you turn into a completely different person."

"You bring it out of me. I love being your little freak," she blushed.

She and Dre had filmed numerous sex tapes. So many that she'd lost count.

"You don't regret filming us having sex do you?"

"No, I love it. It's so uninhibiting."

"I'm glad you said that 'cause if I don't get $100,000 from you by Monday, I'm going to post each tape online one-by-one." Dre said in a menacing tone.

"Boy, stop playing." Kelly laughed thinking he was joking.

Dre stopped in his tracks.

"I never joke about money." He informed her.

"You can't be serious," Kelly said in disbelief.

"It's not a game, love." Dre caressed the side of her face. "You're a sweet girl; you know that? A little gullible, but sweet."

Everything around Kelly went deathly silent. She wasn't being punked. This was real. He was really blackmailing her.

"Why would you do this to me? I thought you loved me?"

"I never told you that. We were just having fun, remember?"

Kelly felt sick. Everything had begun to spin. In front of her were two of Dre instead of one.

"Why are doing this to me?" She asked barely able to breathe.

"'Cause this is what I do, sweetheart."

Kelly immediately began to cry.

"Awww... don't cry. You look ugly when you cry." Dre wiped her face.

"Fuck you!" Kelly slapped his hand away.

"What you mad for? You said you had fun filming. You said you didn't regret it so you shouldn't feel any type of way if I release the tapes, right?"

"You ain't releasing shit!" Kelly hissed.

"Exactly, 'cause you're going to do as I say and give me $100,000, right?" Dre gripped her arm tight. "Right?"

Kelly swallowed the huge lump in her throat. She had no choice but to say yes. She couldn't risk her family and friends or the parents at Jaden Jr.'s preschool seeing her on tape having sex. Everyone would find out she'd been using drugs. She couldn't risk it. She had no way out.

"I'll give you the money," she scowled.

"Good girl." Dre smiled pushing her away.

The next few hours for Kelly were a blur. Somehow she had safely gotten Jaden Jr. from school and back home. Kelly was a nervous wreck. Her entire life had been flipped upside down. Dre had her totally fooled her. How had she not seen this coming? Their whole entire relationship was a game and a set up.

How could you be so stupid, she thought pacing back and forth across her sitting room floor. Kelly's mind was all over the place. She didn't know what to do. She had to figure out a way to get out of this mess without killing Dre. She couldn't risk going to jail for murder but what other choice did she have? It was Friday so she had two more days to come up with a plan.

"Mama, can I have some Cheez-Its," Jaden Jr. asked.

He was sitting on the floor in front of the television watching PBS.

"Sure, baby." Kelly walked into the kitchen and got the box.

She couldn't stop from shaking. Back in the sitting room she handed Jaden Jr. the whole entire box and resumed pacing. She didn't have $100,000 just lying around. Her money was tied up in stocks and bonds. Kelly sat down on the edge of the couch.

"What am I going to do?" She cried. "God, help me."

"What's wrong, mama?" Jaden Jr. asked.

"Nothing, baby," Kelly assured. "Just watch TV ok."

"Ok." Jaden Jr. stuffed a handful of Cheez-Its in his mouth.

Kelly wanted nothing more than to die. Her life was over. *How could you have been so fuckin' stupid?* Flashbacks of her doing coke and having threesomes with Dre and Rico tormented her mind. Her mother would have a heart attack if she saw the footage. Kelly didn't want to think anymore. She needed to escape to wonderland, so she opened her purse.

She needed a line or two to calm her down. Grabbing a magazine, she created two, even lines with an envelope. Kelly rolled up a $100 bill and snorted the two lines of coke. Instantly, euphoria was present. Her whole entire body instantly began to relax. A sky full of stars danced before her eyes. Kelly lay back on the couch. Suddenly she began to laugh. She didn't know why she was laughing but it felt great. Before she knew it, she'd drifted off to sleep.

"KELLY, GET UP!" Jaden yelled in a panic. "GET YO' ASS UP!" He kicked her with his foot.

Kelly stirred around in her sleep but didn't wake up.

"Kelly, get up!" Jaden shook her body profusely.

"Huh? What?" She finally opened her eyes irritated. She had no idea where she was.

"What the fuck is wrong wit' you? You doing coke in front of my fuckin' son?!" Jaden held Jaden Jr. in his arms.

Kelly focused her attention on her son. He had coke residue all over his little face and hands.

"Oh my God!" She screamed. "What have I done? Baby, are you ok?" She tried to take Jaden Jr. from his father's arms but Jaden wouldn't allow it.

"Get the fuck away from him! You'll never touch him again!" He grabbed his car keys.

"Where are you going? Where are you taking my baby?" Kelly sobbed, running after him.

"I'm taking him to the fuckin' hospital!" Jaden shot slamming the door behind him.

Kelly fell into a heap of tears on the floor. Her life had gone from bad to worse to now majorly fucked up.

"Never in my life did I think I'd be picking you of all people up from jail," Meesa teased as Kelly walked out of the building. "I at least thought it would be Destiny or Gwyn."

Kelly had been in jail for the illegal use of drugs and child endangerment for the past 24 hours. After Jaden took Jaden Jr. to the hospital, the police was notified and Kelly was immediately arrested. The only reason she'd been released is because she posted bail.

Jail was not the place for her. It was cold and dirty. The other inmates scared her to death. She couldn't get out of the hellhole fast enough. Jail was the least of her problems though. Child Protective Services had been contacted and now Kelly was in jeopardy of losing custody of her son too. She knew that God didn't place more on a person than they could handle but Kelly was on the brink of losing it. If one more fucked up thing happened she was sure to do something crazy. Kelly got inside of Meesa's G wagon drained.

"Ugh, and you stink." Meesa held her nose. "Let me roll down my damn window." She pressed the down button.

"Not now, Meesa." Kelly said not in the mood for jokes.

"I'm sorry, friend. Are you ok?"

"No. They're gonna take my baby away from me. Meesa, I can't lose my baby," Kelly wept.

"They're not going to take Jaden away from you," Meesa tried to give her friend some hope.

"Then I gotta pay this muthafucka $100,000—"

"Girl, fuck that; we ain't giving that nigga shit!" Meesa cut her off. "We gon' figure something out. We got a day to do it so put your thinking cap on, bitch, and stop crying."

"There's nothing to think about. I'm fucked."

Monday had finally come. Kelly had wished it away but it was still here. She couldn't run from her reality or hide. What was happening was real. Life for her had come full circle. She sat on a bench in Central Park awaiting Dre's arrival. This time, they weren't going to have a steamy encounter under a bridge for all of New York City to see.

This time, she would give him $100,000 in order to keep him from ruining her life. Kelly's palms were sweating as she waited. At any minute she was sure to pass out. She couldn't wait for this to be over so she could move on with her life. It was going on 2:00pm and Dre was nowhere in site. They'd agreed to meet at 1:15pm.

Maybe he'd changed his mind. Kelly prayed that he had. Maybe all of her praying had worked. God was answering her prayers. Dre had come to his senses and decided to leave her alone. She couldn't have been more relieved. She could now breathe freely without feeling like she was going to pass out.

Now all Kelly had to worry about was her court hearing. She could focus all of her energy on not losing her son. Kelly happily stood up and grabbed the briefcase that was sitting next to her. She was just about to walk off when Dre appeared. Her heart immediately dropped down to her knees. Her nightmare wasn't over. It had just begun.

Kelly plopped back down onto the park bench in despair. Dre walked towards her cockier than ever. He didn't have a care in the world. Life for him was great. He was about to become $100,000 richer.

"You didn't think I was coming, did you? Yo' ass got happy there for a second, didn't you?" He joked.

The sight of him made Kelly ill. When she met him for coffee months prior, she'd never envisioned this being their fate. All she was looking for was a release. She thought that the grass would be greener with Dre but in all actuality, he only made her life worse. He'd turned her life into a living hell.

"You look good though. I see you've gone back to dressing like a schoolmarm," he teased picking at her shirt.

Kelly wore a black, cashmere coat, leopard print blazer, black blouse, black trousers and black pointed toe Lanvin pumps.

"Kiss my ass." She jerked away. "Let's just get this over with so I never have to see your face again," she grimaced.

"You ain't hurting my feelings, girl," Dre laughed. "But nah, for real, let's get down to business so I can get outta here. Is it all there?"

"Yes. The $100,000 that you're blackmailing me for is right here." She held up the briefcase. "Do you have what we filmed on a disc?"

"Right here." Dre patted his breast pocket.

"Good." Kelly handed him the briefcase in return for the disc.

"I'm just happy that you didn't fight me on this. I trained you well."

Kelly glared at him with hatred in her eyes. It was taking everything in her not to spit in his face.

"Were you really going to release the tapes against my will if I didn't give you $100,000?" She died to know.

"Yeah. I told you I wasn't playing."

"You could've destroyed my life if those tapes ever got out. But you don't even care, do you?"

"Look, man, we're grown. You knew what you were doing. Nobody forced you to bust it wide open," Dre grinned devilishly.

"You're right. We are grown. That's why my grown ass decided to contact the police." Kelly stood up and revealed the wire that she was wearing.

Dre's eyes grew wide with fear. Before he could escape, a team full of officers swarmed him. Kelly stood frozen watching as they arrested him.

"Get off of me! You have it all wrong! I was just playing with her! It was all a joke!" Dre pleaded.

But his cries went unnoticed. He'd been caught and now he was going to jail.

"You ok, friend?" Meesa came up and hugged Kelly.

"Yeah." Kelly hugged her back. "I'm just happy that this nightmare is finally over."

Epilogue

Kelly had been through hell and back and survived. She'd become addicted to cocaine, blackmailed, arrested, released on bond, lost custody of her son, ordered to rehab and had completed community service. After months of extensive treatment, she was released from rehab. She was now in court standing before a judge begging to gain temporary, joint custody of her son.

Kelly had learned from her mistakes. She'd gone overboard with all of the hard partying and drugs. It was ok to live a quiet normal life. It wasn't ok to use her frustration with her life as an excuse to act out. She was a grown woman. She now knew how to handle her emotions better than she had.

Nothing, not even her happiness, was more important than Jaden Jr. He was priority number one. Somewhere along the lines she'd lost sight of that. Thankfully, Jaden had done a phenomenal job of taking care of him while Kelly was away at rehab. He brought Jaden Jr. to see her every weekend. Kelly was grateful that he had stepped up to the plate when she needed him most. He managed being a full-time dad and holding down a full-time job. Kelly was proud of him. Jaden was finally growing up.

Their relationship was over. They would never get back together. They'd accepted it. It was for the best. They'd only held on so long because of time and loyalty to one another. In the end, their relationship became a game of tug-of-war. She'd lost respect for him and Jaden had lost respect for himself.

But things were different now. Jaden was a new man. He simply wanted what was best for his son, which was his mother. Jaden spoke on Kelly's behalf in court that day. Kelly couldn't have been more grateful for his act of kindness.

Jaden could've been bitter and spiteful towards her for what she'd done but he wasn't. After much deliberation, the judge granted Kelly temporary, joint custody of her son. Kelly cried tears of joy.

Spring was always Gwyn's favorite time of the year. It was like God was breathing new life back into the earth. The sun beamed bright, birds were chirping, people were friendlier. Life was good. Gwyn couldn't have been happier. She was long overdue for some joy. The last six months of her life had been an emotional roller coaster.

Regaining Stevie's trust hadn't been the easiest. They'd gone through hell trying to mend their relationship. After several knock down, drag out arguments, Gwyn demanded that they go to family therapy to sort out their problems. Stevie was against going at first but after a few sessions she started to connect with the therapist.

Since their initial visit, Gwyn had begun to see a significant change in Stevie's behavior. She was still a handful but she'd become a little softer in her delivery and the way she spoke to Gwyn. Plus, she was secretly thrilled that she had a little sister on the way. Gwyn was almost due and scared out of her mind.

She could barely handle Stevie. She didn't know how in the hell she was going to handle a newborn baby too. Thank God she had Cash by her side for the ride. He'd been nothing short of an angel. When they found out Gwyn was pregnant with baby #2 he was surprisingly excited. All of the time he'd missed out on when Stevie was a child he'd now be able to experience with the new baby.

Cash had gone from a bachelor who never wanted kids to a full blown family man. Life for him was a challenge at times but he had Stevie, whom he'd grown to love and adore, his new baby girl on the way and the love of his life Gwyn. They had a whirlwind love affair but he wouldn't erase a moment of it for the world.

Meesa and Black watched gleefully as Mila took the stage for her ballet recital. The two parents couldn't have been prouder. Their baby girl was growing up so fast. Meesa could still vividly remember the day she was born. Life for her was so much simpler then. The world was her oyster. Meesa was bright-eyed and bushy-tailed. Back then she believed that love could conquer all.

Now that she was an adult and had gone through some things, she knew better. In a marriage you needed more than love to survive. You needed to know how to communicate. Respect was a must. Trust had to be established and earned and most importantly, you had to have God at the fore front which she and Black lacked. For years they thought that they could solve their problems on their own but they were sadly mistaken. Black and Meesa needed a higher power to bring them through the storm.

They'd been separated for six months and still lived apart but progress was being made everyday. Black was making a valiant effort to make her see that he was truly sorry for being unfaithful. Meesa knew that he regretted his decision. Every time he had to leave and go home after a visit she could see it in his eyes.

She had to regain her trust in him though. That would take time but now that Victor was back she could let her guard down and breathe some. Meesa was doing everything in her power to involve herself more in Black's life. She'd gone out with him numerous times to the club and even started smoking cigars with him.

Marriage took work. Black and Meesa knew this. They were putting all of their energy into putting theirs back on track. At the end of the day, an undeniable, undisputed love existed between the two of them. She loved him from the moment they met and to him she was the girl with the pretty, hazel-green eyes that had stolen his heart. Nobody had a perfect love story. Black and Meesa were the perfect example of that. No their past wasn't pretty but their future was bright. As long as they had each other, they had nothing to lose.